The Cave in the Rock

Gradie Austin Ewell

Best Wishes to John Thyselie

Gradie Austin Ewell
11-14-17

Copyright

The Cave in the Rock is a work of fiction. All names, characters, locations, and incidents are the products of the author's imagination or are used fictitiously. Any resemblance to actual events, locales, or persons, living or dead, is entirely coincidental.

THE CAVE IN THE ROCK: A NOVEL

Copyright © 2017 by Gradie Austin Ewell

All rights reserved.

Cover Design by KP Designs
Published by Kingston Publishing Company

The uploading, scanning, and distribution of this book in any form or by any means—including but not limited to electronic, mechanical, photocopying, recording, or otherwise—without the permission of the copyright holder is illegal and punishable by law. Please purchase only authorized editions of this work, and do not participate in or encourage electronic piracy of copyrighted materials. Your support of the author's rights is appreciated.

Print ISBN: 978-0-9969540-4-4

Dedication

I am dedicating this book to my husband, Billy Paul Ewell. Thank you for your patience and understanding.

Table of Contents

Copyright 3
Dedication 5
Chapter 1: 9
Chapter 2: 15
Chapter 3: 21
Chapter 4: 27
Chapter 5: 43
Chapter 6: 49
Chapter 7: 53
Chapter 8: 59
Chapter 9: 69
Chapter 10: 77
Chapter 11: 87
Chapter 12: 97
Chapter 13: 107
Chapter 14: 115
Chapter 15: 123
Chapter 16: 131
Chapter 17: 139
Chapter 18: 145
Chapter 19: 151

Chapter 1:
The Picnic and the Hog Killing

Missy and Jake had just finished their picnic, as the sun was hanging low in the West. It had been a very good picnic consisting of biscuit and fried hog jowl and left-over apple pie she had smuggled under her bed the night before.

It had been quite a task to sneak back into the kitchen and wrap the pie in a cloth napkin (she would destroy the evidence tomorrow) and place it into her pantaloons before climbing the long staircase to her bedroom at the top.

She didn't have any trouble getting the sandwiches the next morning after breakfast because there was always left-over biscuits and hog-jowl left in the kitchen cabinet for the children to scarf down about mid-morning when they grew tired and needed a little additional energy. Agnes, the cook had volunteered to pack the picnic basket for her.

As the two of them sat with their stomachs too full, she asked Jake if he knew about the meat they had just devoured. Although Jake did not want to admit he had never given such things a thought in his seven years, he stated he thought he knew, but wanted to know just how much she knew about the meat. So, she shared her story with him. She cautioned him, however, that he must never reveal that she had witnessed the messy, gory awful sight of a hog killing.

It had been decided that a nine-year-old should never witness such a horrible sight, but she knew how to climb trees and get a first-hand look at the goings on.

First the hog would be shot as it ran around the barn yard then lay kicking until the life had left its body.

Next the men would tie the hind legs and hang the hog, head down, on the structure they had built for the occasion. Its throat would be cut to drain the blood and a clean pan would be placed under the head to catch the blood. She knew how delicious 'blood pudding' was (although seeing this process lessened the taste a bit).

A barrel of boiling water was placed in such a position that the hog could be lowered into the it for about ten minutes, then raised from it for the men to scrape the hairs from the flesh. After the flesh had been scraped and cleaned, the stomach was cut open and the entrails removed. The animal would then be placed on a huge table where the dissecting would begin.

First the liver would be saved as well as the heart, then the other various parts would be cut to suit the owner of the hog. The hind quarters would be severed for Hams. The front shoulders would be cut for other prize pieces. Both would be salted heavily and hung in the 'smoke house' to cure. Then there was pork chops, bacon, and tenderloin to be cut into pieces. Most of the head would be boiled and be made into 'head cheese' or 'souse' as it was called. Even the feet of the hog would be boiled and "pickled. They used everything but the 'squeal'," she mused.

She knew that 'Brains combined with Scrambled Eggs' was a breakfast delicacy she loved. It, too, had been a little less tasty after the process had been viewed.

Some of the entrails were cleaned and used to contain the sausage that would be made from some of the meat.

After that, she never wanted to attend another 'hog killing', she told Jake.

Now why did her mind wander to that terrible scene that would be forever stamped on her mind she wondered? Especially today when they were playing her favorite game of "House". She guessed it was because of the hog jowl in the picnic basket.

They had pretended he was the Father and she was the Mother of twin babies. There had been rocks to outline the house, marking spaces for the kitchen where she cooked a delicious meal of bacon, eggs, biscuits and gravy on a make-believe stove and they pretended to have breakfast (by dividing a biscuit) on a large rock laid on another smaller rock for their table. The doors and windows were marked by simply hammering large sticks, on either side, into the ground with another rock. There was, of course, the bedroom where rock beds held the precious twins. They were made from sticks and twigs gathered from around the farm. The girl twin had hair consisting of a piece of lace that Missy had sneaked from the house in her blouse. They named the twins Joseph and Judith.

As the Father, Jake went into the woods and killed a deer for their meat. He made a bow with some string he had brought along in case they would need it. The arrow was a very straight stick. Jake always carried a small whittlin' knife in case he met a bear in the woods. He felt he could defeat any old brown or black bear.

This was to be their secret home forever.

When they had tired of playing house, it was Jake's turn to say what they would do for the rest of the day. He chose 'The Cave in the Rock', which always seemed to have a sort of mystical, magical, scary, aura to Missy. She really didn't want to go there to play, but Jake had been so willing to play her game of 'Pretend' that she didn't feel she should ruin his day by telling him of her misgivings. After all, he had played the part of the Father with much bravery and he had told her of his pretend encounter with a very large bear - but she must never reveal his secret to anyone - which she swore never to do. She even stood with her hand over her heart when she swore this oath.

Upon traveling back to the rear of the cave, they found a large rock where two or three people could hide. It was cooler back there so they came out to the mouth of the cave. She spread the table cloth on the ground once again and finished the last of the picnic food.

Then they sat down on the rocks at the entrance to the cave and watched a barge loaded with corn go down the river.

"You know, Jake, that corn could have come from our farm. It could be going on down to New Orleans for people down there," Missy told him.

Where is New Orleans?" Jake asked her.

"I really don't know but my Father says it's a long way from here," answered Messy.

From their vantage point, they could also see the top of the tin roof of Fisherman Joe's shack.

"Could we go and see Fisherman Joe some time?" asked Jake.

Missy replied, "I guess so. Mother says he is kind of strange though. His wife and kids burned up in a fire in New York and he went almost crazy 'till he came back here and built that shack down by the river."

"Oh, that's right, I remember my Mom talking about it. But I'd still like to go down and visit with him if you're not afraid to," Jake returned.

"He's a nice man. I know because I've gone with Mother to pick up fish for Friday night supper. He looked at me and asked if I would ever want to go fishing. Mother wasn't too keen on the idea, but he told her I would be alright. He can swim in case I would fall in the river", said Missy.

"That settles it!" Jake exclaimed. "We'll go visit him soon."

Jake had no idea how soon that would be.

Suddenly, they realized it was getting dark. Jake acknowledged he might get a scolding for getting home so late, but that if he were sent to bed without supper, he wouldn't care because he was still full of the picnic food and apple pie. So, he left quickly, leaving her to complete the clean-up of the picnic.

Chapter 2:
The Men in the Cave

Missy was startled, then the feeling quickly turned to fear, as she heard several horses coming at a fast pace toward the cave. Panic gripped her very tiny whole body as she thought about what to do. Her instinct told her to run - but to where? As she grabbed the empty picnic basket, she remembered a large hollow rock at the back of the cave and she made a hurried run for the back of the cave where she almost fell and lost her breath. She was shaking with fear!!

    As the horsemen dismounted, she could recognize some of the men's voices. She was able to distinguish the Sheriff John Bolden, a tall lanky man about thirty; the red-headed County Judge, Amos Chandler who was riding his favorite mare, Misty; Sam Whittaker, a short, plump little man who was the owner of the local saloon; Abraham Dunbar the town bully, wearing a mean, surly look on his ugly, scarred face (He liked to brag about the men whose faces he had scarred with his humongous fists); Isaac Merriweather who owned the next farm south of her father's farm, was usually a very good neighbor. Even he looked extremely different in the light of the torches the men were carrying. His face portrayed a man who was very different; and Thomas Jordan the Blacksmith, with huge arms and dark, curly hair. His face seemed to bear the look of anger, yet, sorrow for the young man in front of the men.

From her vantage point, in the darkened cave, Missy could see their faces and could not believe the evil looks those most respected Men of the community wore on them. She had never seen a devil but these men looked as if they were in cahoots with him. Then there was another man, a seventh man. This man's hands were tied behind him, and was being almost dragged into the cave. In shock and disbelief, she recognized him because he was her School Teacher, Mr. Theodore Schnell. Why was this scene taking place? He must have done some horrible thing to be brought to this secret place for punishment.

"I guess you know why we've brought you here?" Isaac Merriweather thundered.

"No, I really don't, but I suspect it has something to do with your daughter," answered Mr. Schnell quietly.

"You're damn right it is," said Merriweather.

"I love Edwina Williams and would never do anything…"

"Shut up!!! I'll do the talking," roared Merriweather. "I don't want you near my daughter. Do you hear me?"

"I hear you, but I don't understand what's going on. I thought everything was alright. You approved of my marriage to Edwina", croaked the scared school teacher who by this time realized what a predicament he was in. It appeared to him that no one here was going to try to help him.

Well, it ain't. Rumor has been going around that you have another girl pregnant in Pope County. That rumor has come plenty straight to this group of men.

"Ain't that right Boys?" Merriweather shouted. All the men present nodded in agreement.

The schoolteacher's face went dead white as if he had seen a ghost. He started to protest but the other man held up his hand to silence him.

"Now, Boy, I'm a fair man." Merriweather lowered his voice, "But I aim to protect my daughter. Ain't that right Boys?" This time the men all voiced their agreement.

Judge Amos Chandler chimed in, "If it was my daughter, I doubt if I would be that kind to this type of low life skunk"

The teacher again tried to defend himself, "I don't even know anyone in Williams County. I never travel there."

The Sheriff said quietly, "That's not what the young Lady said. She said it happened on the night of the Allegany River Dance. That you invited her to go walking with her and a little piece into the woods, you threw her to the ground and raped her. She was so ashamed she wasn't going to say anything but she turned up pregnant. No sir, Abagail Henning named you as the father. Her father would have made you marry her, but she cried and begged him not to. The baby will be given away."

Once more the teacher tried to deny the lie to no avail.

Merriweather continued in his low toned voice: "Now, Boy, I'm giving you a chance. I'm givin' you $100 dollars and you can keep your horse when you go. You will leave this place tonight. You will not go home and get anything. You will not speak to anyone until you are at least 100 miles from here. And…you will never, in any way, try to contact my daughter again. Do you understand?"

The Teacher gulped and quietly uttered, "I believe I do".

Merriweather intoned, "Have you ever seen a body after it's been in the water for a week? After it's swelled and bloated and risen to the surface?"

The Teacher barely spoke, "No, sir".

Amos Dunbar sneered, "H'it shore h'ain't a purty sight. I'd shore hate to see you end up like that." (Then he chuckled a low laugh)

The Teacher said shakily, "Mr. Merriweather, you will never see me again…I promise. I hope you can live with what you are forcing me to do."

"Hell, boy," Merriweather roared. "I'll sleep a lot better tonight, knowing you're gone for good and can't ever touch my daughter again. Now, get going before I change my mind and do what I really want to do to you."

After the Blacksmith untied the Teacher's hands, he strode from the Cave, mounted his horse and everyone could hear the horse running away at the fastest gait possible.

The men strode silently from the Cave and rode away.

As they rode away, Missy heard Merriweather ask, "Did I do the right thing?"

One of the men answered, "I'd have killed him!!!"

Missy's heart was still pounding as she waited to be sure the men were gone. By this time, she could hardly see her way out of the Cave.

She felt she would never be able to tell anyone, except Jake and Fisherman Joe, what she had seen and heard tonight.

Chapter 3:
Fisherman Joe and the Shack Down by the River

Missy did not sleep well that night after seeing the men in the cave threaten her teacher will killing him if he ever came back to this county. When she did sleep, she had terrible nightmares.

The next morning, she could hardly wait for Jake to come over to play. Why was he always so slow? Maybe she would have to go over to his house and see if something was wrong.

Missy ate the oatmeal, toast and finished off her glass of milk in a hurry. She wanted to be ready when Jake finally got there.

"Have I got something to tell you," she whispered quietly rushing him off the porch.

Her eyes were huge as she told him this.

She motioned him to follow her out of earshot from the house.

"Now," she said in a hushed voice. "You must hold your hand over your heart and swear 'Cross my heart and hope to die. Jesus told me not to lie'."

Curiosity got the best of Jake and he did as he was told.

He listened intently as she spun the tale of what happened the night before and his eyes grew with excitement and fear.

She told him of how she almost fell trying to get behind the big rock in the back, who the men were and how their teacher rode away as fast as he could go.

When she stopped to catch her breath, he began his questions.

"Why were the men so mad? Did she think the men would have beat up or killed the Teacher and throw him in the river?"

"I don't know, but we need to talk to someone who might have the answers," she said.

Suddenly. Jake had an idea, "I know who we can talk to – Fisherman Joe."

"That's right, he would be able to tell us all about it," she replied.

They made their way toward the river and the cave.

Fisherman Joe lived in a shack down by the river. He had made it from old boards as they floated down the river. The rest he would find at the local dump. It didn't look too fancy, but it was large enough for a kitchen and another room he called his 'livin' room. When the river flooded, he moved what he could up to the cave and lid in there until the water receded. Sometimes. The water got so high he would have to leave the cave and go to even higher ground. That was how the names got on the ceiling of the cave.

When he was young, he was about 6 feet tall, but life had reduced him down to 5' 10 inches. The cares of life caused him to stoop. His wife and three children perished in a hotel fire while they were in New York visiting kin folk. He had left to go buy smokes at the store when it happened. When he returned the entire hotel was in flames. For a while he wandered the country trying to find himself. He stumbled on the cave in the rock and stayed for three months. The river, with its barges, boats and gentle lapping at the shore seemed to sooth his harried nerves enough for him to remain there. Now he was content just to mend his nets and catch enough fish to give him sufficient money to buy supplies he needed.

Mother Martha always bought the fish for the Williams family from Fisherman Joe. He saved the best spoon billed catfish for her. He would cut the fish fillets and steaks just the way she liked them. A majority of the town bought their fish from him too.

Right now, the river was still within its banks. Fisherman Joe was sitting in front of his shack mending the nets when Missy and Jake arrived.

"Mornin' Youngin's. How are you this fine morning?" said Fisherman Joe. "Ya'll look exhausted. Have you been running?"

Jake caught his breath first and blurted out, "Mister Jose, have we got something to tell you!"

"Well it must be exciting for you to be in such a hurry to get here so out of breath," he stated.

Missy finally caught her breathe and tried to be calm.

"Oh, Mister Joe, I really almost got scared to death last night," she said. Recalling the previous night she spun the story about the men in the cave and how they treated the school teacher. She said she reckoned the he didn't stop until he was a hundred miles from there.

"I know all about it," Fisherman Joe said. "I heard the horses come running in fast. I crept up the bank so I could hear what all the commotion was about. Now, I don't believe the Teacher had anything to do with that girl. He's just not that kind of man. There's no use fighting against the Sheriff and the Judge. That big bully was aching to beat up the teacher, and the teacher knew it. He chose the only option he could do, poor man."

"I have to tell you," he continued. "This is not the only time that group has brought a man to the cave and rendered judgement on him. There was the case of James Harding who was accused of stealing a horse from the Judge. He swore he didn't go near the mare, but couldn't convince the men that night. They gave him a choice, leave town and not return or be killed and thrown in the river. Of course, like teacher, he left town.

"It's not right," Missy said. "Everyone should be given a chance to tell their side of the story."

"I feel like you, but what can you do when you have some of the most influential men in town throwing a mock trial within the cave?" asked Fisherman Joe.

The two children finally said that they wanted to go fishing in the river. Fisherman Joe didn't give into them and take them out on the boat he had tied up at the river bank. They were overjoyed to catch several small fish that day anyways.

Missy gave all the fish she caught and he kept saying, "Boy my mom will be so happy to get these fish to cook."

As Fisherman Joe watched the two children go, he had a frown on his face. He really hoped they would keep the pledge they made that day. If not, it could mean big trouble for him.

Chapter 4:
Vigilantes

Missy didn't keep her promise to stay away from the cave. Late that same night, she sneaked back close to the mouth of the cave and waited to see if the group of men, who had threatened her teacher, would be back.

Her quest did not have to wait too long. The same group of men came riding together with another man in tow.

It was a man known to be the town Barber. His name was James Followel and, as far as she knew, was a very good and respected man. His hands were tied in front of him and he was tied to the saddle horn.

From her vantage point, she watched the entire scene.

The Judge was the first to speak.

"Now James, as I recall, you threatened to cut Sheriff Boldin's throat because he told you he didn't feel he needed to pay you for haircuts and shaves." The words were spoken with righteous indignation by the Judge.

The terrified barber spoke, "That's not exactly true. I just wanted to let him know I held his life in my hands. I need every penny I earn to take care of my family. I merely nicked the side of his face back by his ear. I.. I.. promise never to do anything like that again to any of you men. Just don't kill me. My family needs me." By this time, he had been able to get down from the horse and was on his knees begging for his life. With his hands tied, the man was defenseless.

The Sheriff took over, "I had a tough time explaining to my wife that I let a damn, no good Barber put a cut on my face and didn't do anything about it. You won't get a chance to do that again." With that said, the Sheriff took out his gun and hit the man hard across his right cheek, leaving a cut about three inches long

"I promise I won't and I'll give you whatever you need done. A shave, haircut, trim your fingernails or toenails. I wouldn't dream of charging any of you fellows. Just give me another chance," he begged.

Sam Whittaker, local saloon owner, now kicked the man in the side and laughed "I'll bet you would. You know, I didn't like the last hair cut you did on me, either. Go ahead and rough him up a bit," he said to Abraham Dunbar, who was known around town to beat up a man just because the man looked back at him.

Abraham Dunbar took immense pleasure in hitting and kicking the Barber who was on his knees. So much that soon the man was a bloody mess and could no longer stand. His hands were still tied so that he could not defend himself and the town bully had a heyday with him.

After the barber had been beaten into unconsciousness, the Bully turned to the other men. "What do you want me to do with him now?" he asked.

"Looks like we'll have to dump him in the river like the others. Untie his hands so they won't suspect anything wrong when they find him down river," said the Sheriff.

At that moment Missy felt a hand on her shoulder. She started to scream but someone put a hand over her mouth.

"I thought you promised to stay away from here at night," whispered Fisherman Joe in her ear. "Stay here. "I have to rescue the Barber when they throw him in the river." With that said, he was gone.

Missy watched as the strong Bully Abraham easily lifted the limp body of the Barber, carried it down to the river and threw it in.

She did not hear the soft easy splash when Fisherman Joe joined the body and swam with it to the river bank.

The men were laughing as they rode away, "He won't want to nick anyone else's throat, will he?" they laughed again.

After they were out of earshot, Missy quickly made her way down to Fisherman Joe's shack. The door was fastened from the inside so that she had to knock and tell him that it was her.

The Barber was lying on the kitchen table moaning, but at least he was breathing.

Fisherman Joe was cutting his shirt off to see if he had broken bones. Sure enough, his right arm was broken and hanging down in a grotesque way. He moaned and Joe put a clean cloth into his mouth. "Bite down on this while I set that arm" said Joe.

He straightened the Barber's arm, put two pieces of wood on each side of the arm and told Missy to hold them while he wrapped strips of cloth around the arm to hold it in place. Joe had some salve for most of the cuts, but sewed up the cut that the Sheriff's gun had made.

Missy was astounded at the way Fisherman Joe was taking care of the Barber. "Where did you learn to do all that?" she asked.

"Now, don't you go telling anyone about this, but I was a Doctor before the fire took my family. Now, I just want to fish and help folks when I can. This isn't the first man I've pulled from the river after those men threw them in. I was able to save all four of the men they beat up and threw into the river," stated Fisherman Joe. "I'll let him stay here and get well. Then when his wife comes to buy fish on Friday, I'll let her know and they can plan their escape. I guess that's my good deeds and I hope the Good Lord sees what I've done enough to get me into Heaven and forgive me for leaving my family in the hotel to die."

"It wasn't your fault. How could you have known the hotel would catch fire? You must not blame yourself," she exclaimed.

"Now, remember, you must not give away my secret, alright?" he asked.

Missy replied, "I will not tell anyone. I must go home now. Hopefully, no one has gone to my room and found me not there." With that statement, she turned and made her way back to her home.

Due to the hour of her arrival at home, Missy decided to wait until morning to tell her Father about what was going on at the Cave in The Rock down by the river.

Next morning, while sitting at the breakfast table. Missy asked innocently, "Are you going to be busy all day today, Father?"

"Why do you ask?"

"Oh, I thought I would go with you to the field. It's so exciting to see the fields of corn being harvested. Jake and I saw a barge loaded with corn yesterday on its way down stream," she replied.

"I'll be leaving for the fields in about 10 minutes. Can you be ready by then?"

"I'm ready right now," Missy told her Father.

As they rode away from the house, Missy told her Father of the real reason she wanted to ride to the fields. That she had something important to tell him.

They dismounted and sat under a large tree.

"Now, little Missy, just what could be so secretive that you couldn't tell me in front of the others at the breakfast table?" asked her Father.

Missy began by telling him about how she was in the cave when the men made the School Teacher leave the county. She named all the men who were in the group.

"I feel so guilty about knowing this when I see how much Edwina cries at night and I can't tell her what happened," said Missy. Then she told him about last night and how the Barber was beaten and thrown in the river to drown.

"Fisherman Joe saved him from the river," she said. "And he's going to hide the Barber until his wife comes to buy fish on Friday. Then the Barber and his wife can make their plans to leave here."

"You're telling me that this has been going on for some time?"

"Yes. Those men are not doing right, are they?" Missy asked.

"No, they are not. Let's go back to the house. I've got some thinking to do about this situation," said Father.

After she and her Father got back to the house, he rode away fast.

Later that day, he and several other local farmers paid a visit to the local Blacksmith, Thomas Jordan.

"Evening, gentlemen, what can I do for you?" Jordan queried.

"We would like an account of where you were last night when James Followel, the Barber, was enticed from his home on the pretense someone was getting married tomorrow and needed a haircut," said Missy's Father.

The man stammered a bit, then said, "Why, I was home. Just ask my wife."

"No, you weren't," said Tom Keeling, another farmer. "You were in the cave where the Barber was beaten unconscious then thrown in the river."

"I don't know what you're talking about. I tell you I was home. Just ask my wife," the blacksmith almost yelled.

"Your wife would only lie for you," said another farmer.

Missy's Father got so close to the Blacksmith that only the other farmers could hear him.

"We have several witnesses who will testify as to what went on at the cave last night. They can name all the men who were there and what was done to the Barber. They have witnessed other such goings on, too," said Missy's Father.

By this time, the blacksmith's eyes were wide and his face was white as a sheet.

"We will call in some of the higher Judges and all of you who are involved in this unholy, murderous act will hang from the new gallows we will build. Do you understand? Now, better still, maybe some quiet night someone will lure you away from your home and take you to the cave and render judgment on you," whispered Missy's father. The other men with him voiced their approval of what he had told the blacksmith.

It just so happened that Abraham Dunbar, town bully, was coming out of the hardware store. Missy's Father hailed him down and asked to speak with him. He ambled over and asked, "Now just what can you be wanting from me?"

"Where were you last night after 10:00 o'clock?"

"None of your damn business. Want to make something of it?" the Bully asked.

"Someone told me you were at the cave last night with some other fellows with a man who you beat within an inch of his life and then you threw him in the river. Any truth to that?" Her father looked the bully straight in the eye.

"Ain't a damn word of it so."

"You know, that's not what the Blacksmith said," he turned to the men with him, "What do you think, boys?" At this, one of the men with him spoke up and said, "I kind of believe that Abraham was there at the cave last night."

Abraham looked as if he had seen a ghost.

"I believe I would be thinking about how, on some dark night, a group of men could waylay you and take you to the cave, my friend," commented Missy's Father. "Yessiree, that just might happen. Now if that man you almost killed last night dies, we just might have to try you for murder. They hang men around here for murder, don't they fellows?" They left the Bully looking scared.

They turned their horses around and headed for the Saloon. When they walked thru the door, Sam Whittaker met them with a smile.

"Can I get you a drink, boys?" he asked.

"We're not here to drink, Sam, we want to know where you were last night after ten o'clock," said Missy's Father.

"Why, I was right here, cleaning up the place. Henry over there can vouch for that." He motioned to the bartender who looked scared but didn't want to lose his job. "Tell them Henry."

"Y..Y..Yes, he was here 'till around midnight," the shaking Bartender barely spoke.

"Now I know you want to keep your job, Henry, but I have it on good authority, from witnesses, that Sam here wasn't here during that time at all, but he was in the cave with some other low-down skunks. Abraham Dunbar almost killed a man namely James Followell. If James dies, the witnesses are prepared to testify that your boss was there and is implicated in the murder. Now Sam, you remember, that we hang people for murder."

"But I didn't touch the barber. Abraham is the one who beat him so badly and threw him in the river. I'm innocent," blurted out the saloon keeper.

"All the same, you better hope he doesn't die," said Missy's father. "It might come down to his word against yours as to who killed him. If I understand correctly, from the witnesses, you kicked him. That might be part of the argument against you, if he dies."

"Boys, if you'll not let this go any further, I won't go near that cave again. I swear it on my mother's grave. I won't be a part of anything like this again. I really didn't want to go last night but the Sheriff told me he would make up something that would close me down if I didn't go," the trembling saloon keeper almost whispered.

"We'll be seeing you later if James dies," said one of the other farmers.

Their next stop was at the jail where Sheriff John Bolden was busy cleaning his six guns to get the blood off from where he had hit James Follower the night before.

"You fellows look like you're on a mission. How can I help you?" asked the Sheriff.

"Did you happen to be working near the Cave in the Rock last night and notice something you felt was not, quite right?" asked Missy's Father.

"Matter of fact, I was riding by and saw some light up by the cave, but figured it was a drinking party and since I was by myself, chose not to go up there," the Sheriff lied.

"Now, that is not what we were told by some witnesses. They told a whole different story. In fact, they said you were in the cave when the town Barber was almost beaten to death and then thrown into the river by Abraham Dunbar and you were the one who told Dunbar to go ahead and throw the body in the river after you finally untied his hands." another of the farmers said.

(By this time the other men were beginning to speak up.)

"What witnesses? Did the others tell you this? Why those dirty rotten liars! I wasn't near the cave last night," he lied again.

"Oh yes you were," said Judge Amos Chandler.

The Judge walked on into the Sheriff's office. "I was there trying to stop the whole sordid thing, but I was outnumbered by the other five men. They took matters into their own hands and I felt so sorry for the barber. His hands were tied so he couldn't even try to defend himself. Yes, it was a terrible sight when Abraham finished beating him up. I tried to stop them, but, as I said, I was one against five. Such a shame," the Judge shook his head.

The sheriff jumped up with his gun drawn. "Why you are lying sack of shit! You were there alright, but you were part of the gang, not trying to get Abraham to stop beating the barber!" the Sheriff roared. "Don't come in here so high and mighty like it wasn't your idea in the first place. You convinced us all that it would save the county money to have these night meetings and administer justice at the cave instead of a legal trial."

The Judge turned to the group of farmers. Are you going to take his word against mine? Who do you think is telling the truth?" asked the Judge.

Missy's Father looked at both men. "You are both lying to save your own skin. I know because I have witnesses to last night's meeting at the cave. Now, here's what is going to happen. First, Sheriff, you are going to resign right now. It appears you do not know the difference between a fair trial and vigilante justice. Put your weapon and your badge on the desk. DO IT NOW!!

The Sheriff thought for minute. "Well, I guess it's time for me to leave and look for some new land in the West." He laid down the weapon and badge and exited the room quickly, leaving the Judge to face the men.

"Please don't let this one time...," the Judge began.

"There have been other times," stated Missy's father. "I believe about four others, not counting the time you made a respected Teacher leave."

"He had raped a girl. He was lucky we let him go," said the Judge.

"He had a right to a fair trial, Judge, you know that," said Missy's father.

"You have me there. I guess I just wanted justice to be done. I'm sorry I got so involved with trying to get things done quickly. So many criminals get off and never serve the time in jail that they deserve."

He looked searchingly at the men. "Are you going to make me give up being the Judge of the County?" he asked.

"We will leave that up to your conscience. Rest assured we have witnesses that could take away your Judgeship any time you do not follow the law."

The Judge hung his head and went out the door.

The last man they visited was Isaac Merriweather, the Farmer.

As they rode up, he came out to meet them. "I know why you're all here and I am so ashamed. When I was invited to go to the cave with the other men I was very glad. I knew they were the most influential men in the County and I felt very proud to have been invited to their ritual in the cave. When I got there, I realized I didn't want to be part of the meeting, but it was too late. By going, I could not quit. So, I had to keep going to keep from becoming one of their victims. I couldn't sleep for feeling so sorry for the victims. Fellows, I am so very sorry. Have you visited all the other men? What did they say? I never did touch any of the men who were brought there for punishment. I didn't have to. Abraham so much enjoyed breaking bones and hearing them beg. I will never do anything like that again, I swear," said the man.

The Farmer was Amish and had been a good neighbor.

"Why didn't you come and tell the rest of us?"

"I was afraid of what they would do to me or my family. I guess you think I'm a coward," the Farmer said. "And I guess I proved that I was and am."

"Any among us would probably have done the same," said Andrew Farthing, another farmer.

"Missy's Father addressed the group of men who had been with him during the afternoon. "I want to thank all of you for coming with me this afternoon. I believe our work is done. This is one day I will never forget. The evil things done at the cave are at an end, I believe. Now, let's go to our homes and keep the events of the day secret to ourselves. It will be interesting to see what our esteemed Judge chooses to do. Goodbye."

As usual, on Friday, the Barber's wife came for fish. She and the Barber cried together as they made plans to leave the area.

Fisherman Joe helped them as much as he could. He changed the dressings on the wounds of the Barber and advised him not to be lifting anything heavy. The Barber's wife would load the wagon as much she could, with the help of the children, and come for him next Friday at noon.

They were all unaware of the visit to the blacksmith and others of that murderous band, that there would be no more meetings at the cave. In fact, the Sheriff resigned and left town stating he wanted to go on westward and stake out a claim on new land. The town bully also left for parts unknown, stating he never liked the people of the town anyway.

As for the Judge, he was home most nights with his wife who was happy about the change in her husband.

Fisherman Joe didn't have to rescue anymore men who had been thrown into the river.

Chapter 5:
Cousin Abagail Henning's Visit

Excitement was at a fever pitch concerning cousin Abagail Henning's coming to the Williams Farm for a visit! She was one of the most beautiful young ladies in Lancaster County and was also extremely talented in both piano and voice. It was being whispered about the area that she was to give a recital as soon as she could get settled in and the affair could be arranged.

The wagon containing the beloved cousin and her personal belongings arrived mid-morning. Cousin Abagail stepped daintily down from the wagon amid loving hugs and greetings.

An elaborate brunch had been prepared for her. Of course, all the Williams family were invited to join her in the delicious repast. The scalloped potatoes, bacon, ham, poached eggs along with fluffy biscuits and tender scones with whipped butter and all kinds of jellies and jams, made fresh there on the farm, were served in beautiful glass dishes.

As Abagail entered the front door, delicious smells wafted from the dining room. At first, she smiled and remarked how delicious the food smelled, but before she could enter the lovely room from whence the fragrance came, she stopped and put her hand to her mouth.

"Oh, I am so sorry", she stammered, "but the ride from home to here has upset my stomach. I have just recently gotten over the stomach flu and it still affects me when the fragrance of food is present. Please forgive me if I do not join you for the lovely brunch you have so graciously prepared for me. I need to lie down and rest from the long journey."

Martha Williams put a loving arm around her and ushered her upstairs to the lovely room reserved for special guests such as Cousin Abagail.

Presently, Martha reappeared and advised that Cousin Abagail would be resting for a while and asked that Cook take a tall glass of iced sweet tea and two pieces of buttered toast up to the room where Abagail would be staying. She asked the rest of the Williams family to go to the dining room and enjoy the wonderful brunch. No sense wasting perfectly wonderful food! She was sure their guest would be feeling perfectly fine by Suppertime.

She wasn't. Cousin Abagail was still feeling the effects of the long journey and begged to be excused again.

Next morning at breakfast, at which Abagail still did not appear, Mother Martha told those present that Abagail's stomach ailment had reappeared and she had taken to her bed for the time being. Her meals would be taken to her room at the top of the stairs. No one was to venture into the room because that it might be contagious. This meant everyone except Cook, who would take meals to her and Mother Martha.

Next day, Mother told the family that she had asked Doctor McMillan to come to the farm to visit both she and Cousin Abagail. Mother, herself had not been feeling well and had been nauseated for several mornings. She was concerned that she, too, might be coming down with the stomach flu.

As was expected, the very next morning, Doctor McMillan showed up at the crack of dawn. He was very prompt in his visits and especially to the Williams farm. They always paid in silver dollars instead of chickens and garden products.

He was frowning when he came out of the bedroom where Abagail was residing. He also examined and questioned Martha concerning the condition of the first patient. When he left, Martha had a stern look on her face as she addressed the rest of the family. "Cousin Abagail's condition is very, very serious. She must be confined to her room for quite some time - possibly some months."

What about you, Martha," asked the concerned husband. "I saw you go into the room with the Doctor, also. Are you going to be alright, or do you also have the stomach flu as Abagail has?"

"I don't really know right now. Time will tell the tale" Martha returned. "For now, be advised that no one can go to Abagail's room, not even you two girls". She looked at both Missy and Edwina with such love, it brought tears to the two sister's eyes as they saw the concern in their mother's. They knew there was more to the story than what she was sharing with them.

Missy walked quickly to her bedroom to try to reason out the thoughts that had been puzzling her. That night, in the Cave, Sheriff John Bolden had said Abagail was pregnant. Were pregnant women always sick at their stomachs? And didn't their stomachs always get huge? Abagail had been nauseous and had stomach flu - or so she told everyone. Now Mother was having morning sickness. Was she pregnant also? It might be nice to have a baby around to play with. Or would she be stuck with taking care of the baby every day? Missy was really confused now.

Missy also had another puzzle. Although it was not a puzzle. Edwina had been asked to teach at the local school now that Theodore Schnell had disappeared. It was a paradox to Missy for she knew that Mr. Schnell had not simply disappeared, but had been forced to leave the County. However, there was no way to go to the authorities because they were the men who caused him to leave town for parts unknown.

What made it even worse was the fact that he and Edwina were to become engaged and announce it at Christmas time.

She had heard Edwina sobbing last night and had gone to Edwin's room to try to comfort her. There was no consoling her sister. Edwina's eyes were all puffy from crying and as she sobbed her story to Missy. She thought her own heart would break for her sister's grief. But she dared not reveal the story of the night in the Cave in the Rock.

The next morning at the breakfast table, Missy thought she detected a strained atmosphere between her Mother and her Father. Mother's eyes looked as if she had been crying and Father was very matter-of-fact when he spoke to her. Missy ate hurriedly and ran outside to see if her playmate had arrived yet. Jake was sometimes late and it never bothered her, but today, she was impatient for him to arrive so she could think of something else rather than the coolness at the breakfast table.

As the weeks passed, Cousin Abagail continued to stay in her room at the top of the stirs. Mother continued to spend a great deal of time with her.

All at once Missy noticed that her mother's stomach was beginning to protrude. As the weeks passed, her Mother's stomach grew and grew. So that was the reason for her father's sudden change of heart. He continued the harshness of his voice when he spoke to Missy's Mother.

One-night Missy happened to be behind the couch in the library reading one of her favorite books when her Father and Mother came into the room together.

"Can't you just go along with the charade until the baby is born?" cried her mother.

"Do I have a choice? You've been wearing that pillow for months, pretending you are pregnant, when it's Abagail who is going to have the baby," her father retorted.

"Yes, Abagail is going to have a baby, but we both agreed, or so I thought we agreed, that we would pretend I am pregnant and that we would give the baby a name and home." said her mother, in a quiet tone. "Abagail's life would be ruined if other people knew she had a baby out of wedlock."

"You are right, as usual, Martha," whispered her father. "I cannot stand to see you unhappy. As far as I can see, we will have another little face in our house to love and cherish as our own child."

Missy could hear the rustle of her Mother's dress as they embraced each other in love as they always had.

Chapter 6:
The Birthing

Then came the day when the labor of child birth began. The Doctor hurried in his carriage making the poor horse run all the way to the Williams farm. Mother was in the bedroom with Abagial, pretending it was she who was having the baby. Abagial was in intense pain that comes with the final throes of giving birth. She clenched a washcloth between her lovely perfect teeth to keep from scramming in pain. Mother sat beside her, kept placing a cold washcloth her head and encouraged her to breathe deeply.

Missy was driven to Melody Smith's house to play until after the baby was born. She pretended she did not know why she was having to be away from home while the excitement of the birthing of the baby was completed. They might as well have let her stay at home during this time, though, because she knew all about it. A month ago, a baby calf was born at the farm and Missy had seen the whole thing. She had watched the calf emerge from its Mother and felt a profound pity for the poor cow. However, Missy did not believe a baby would be able to try to stand as soon as it was born, like the baby calf did.

She was invited to remain at Melody's home until the next day. It was alright to play with dolls and doll houses for a while, but she was bored after a while and longed to just go outside and climb a tree. However, she was not bored enough to suggest they go back to the Cave in the Rock. She carefully avoided that place since that night when her teacher barely escaped with his life.

Back at the William's farm the doctor was busy with the details of delivering the tiny baby girl. She emerged as Abagail gave the last hard push and lay against the sweat dampened pillow. The tiny baby girl was born with a head full of red, curly hair. Mother carried the little infant over to the wash basin to clean the tiny face and body. She began putting on the waiting clothes when Abagail gave another heart-wrenching cry. When the doctor quickly turned to look at the new mother, he was astonished. He could see she was giving birth to a second baby.

The doctor immediately began preparations to deliver the second child. He encouraged Abagail to rest between the labor pains. He wanted her to save the strength for each agonizing push. Abagail tried valiantly to do as the doctor advised, but at long last, her strength was gone.

The doctor shouted to mother, "Lay that baby down and come quickly. We don't want to lose this other baby. Stand above her head. The next time she has a pain and tries to push, place your hands on her stomach and push the baby down as far as you can to help expel the baby."

Mother Martha ran to Abagail's bed and did as the doctors' ordered.

After about thirty minutes of pushing and waiting the tiny boy child was born. The doctor smacked him on his rear several times. He did not catch his breath nor cry. In desperation the doctor yelled, "bring a basin of very warm water and a basin of icy water. Hurry!"

Within minutes the basins of water were placed on the bed. Immediately the doctor dipped the infant into the chilly water first followed by the warm water. At the third dip into the freezing water the baby caught his breath and whimpered.

The doctor grabbed a bloody towel and wrapped the child in it to retain whatever warmth that was possible for the baby. The infant continued to whimper but he did not cry as his sister had done.

As the doctor sat, holding him, he spoke to the baby. "Well, I wasn't sure we would be holding a dead or alive child right now, but you fooled us all. God bless you, sweet little boy. You made it."

The doctor gave the baby boy to Mother and went to Abagail's bedside. "Well child," he said. "You have given birth to two fine babies. I am very proud of you."

Abagail turned her face to the wall and spoke between sobs, "but I'll never be able to claim them as my own. I'll always have to pretend they belong to my friend."

When Missy finally got home, everyone was so busy hurrying to and from Mothers bedroom. Missy took the stairs two at a time and rushed in to see the new baby. But what a surprise! There were two of them. The tiny baby boy was lying in the cradle where all the Williams children had lain and Mother was holding the little baby girl in her arms.

Missy's eyes grew wide with surprise. She ran to her Mother's bed and gave her a great big hug and kiss. She knew these two innocents would never take her place in Mothers heart.

As she gazed at the sleeping babies her heart melted. After all, it isn't every day that you get a new brother and sister.

Chapter 7:
Jonathan

The babies grew as the weeks went by. Mother chewed food then put it into the infants' mouths as was the custom in 1837.

"They were growing like weeds," Mother Martha commented.

The whole county seemed to want to visit the Williams's home to see the two tiny wonders. The tiny blonde boy was getting fatter, but not as much as his red-headed sister. He was quiet while she demanded attention.

After several invitations to dinner at other homes in the area, it was time for the Williams to host another fabulous meal at their home.

Among the usual guests were the Sheriff and wife; the Judge and wife; the Saloon Keeper and wife, and several close friends. It was a jolly occasion and everyone was very happy to have been invited to the dinner.

The babies were on display in all their finery and Mary Lee Chandler simply could not keep her hands off the little ones. She almost cried when she touched the tiny infants. Her heart was broken to know she would never be able to birth a child. Likewise, her husband was mesmerized by the twins. He even got down on his hands and knees and tried to get them to laugh. The tiny boy only stared at him, but the rowdy little girl laughed out loud. This pleased the Judge so very much that he had trouble eating without looking at her.

Country fried chicken, whipped potatoes, gravy, sweet corn on the cob, fresh green beans from the garden, fried okra, a huge blackberry cobbler, chocolate cake, heavy whipped cream for the cobbler, and of course, delicious hot rolls with splendid strawberry butter. Yes, the Williams had a wonderful cook.

After dinner, the men retired to the smoking room where the subject of war between the States was discussed. They all agreed that the South must not be permitted to secede from the Union. None of them wanted to start a war, but, if it came to that they would be for it. Father stated "Well, if a war is started, they will need Doctors. I surely hope they don't take Jonathan, my son."

As the guests left, once again Abagail looked from her window above and cursed the man who had raped her. She never wanted to lay eyes on him again. It was time to go home. Tears came to her eyes as she thought of leaving her babies but sooner or later she must make the decision to leave them. 'I can still come to visit them' she thought.

The next morning, Abagail appeared at the breakfast table with red swollen eyes and announced she would be going home tomorrow. Everyone made comments about how she could stay if she wanted and why did she feel she should go home now?

Mother said she could understand that Abagail needed to get on with her life and she would have the wagon ready in the morning for the journey. It didn't look as if it would be raining tomorrow.

Suddenly the front door was flung open and a loud holler was emitted from a voice familiar to the family, but the family had not heard for two years! The William's only son, Jonathan, had returned from England where he had been studying at Oxford College to be a Medical Doctor. His handsome face had a smile that relayed how happy he was to be home again.

"Where is breakfast?" he called. "I'm starved for the good breakfast at home. Those English cooks don't know how to make a "sunny side up egg", and what they call biscuits - well you'd better not drop them on your toe."

After the surprise wore off, everyone rushed to hug and kiss the long-lost son! They rushed so fast, he almost fell during their happy welcome!

Only Cousin Abagail remained at the table. She could not take her eyes off the handsome young man who had just created havoc during the breakfast. Her heart skipped several beats and when she caught her breath, she still could not utter a word.

Presently, after Jonathan had been seated, he noticed the beautiful young woman sitting across from him at the table.

"Well… hello there," he said, "and where have you been all my life?"

"This is Cousin Abagail," Mother said. "She's been with us for a while, but just announced this morning she would be going back to her parent's home in the morning."

"That's a shame. Here I just got home and you're leaving. Now just how far away do you live?" Jonathan questioned.

At his obviously joking manner, Abagail was stunned for a moment but regained her composure quickly.

"Too far for you to ride in an hour. I am sure you will be too tired to make such a long journey very soon," she retorted.

"Well! She has spirit! I love that! Sorry if I offended you dear Lady, I was merely making conversation," he said.

With that, she asked to be excused, stating she had a lot to pack for the 'long journey home' tomorrow.

When she was out of earshot, Jonathan asked about her. "How long had she been here? Why she stayed so long? What had made her want to go home now? Who is she?"

"It's a long story and I'll tell you all about it presently," Mother said. "But now, 'eat drink and be merry' we are so glad to have you return from England. It seems like years since you left and we have missed your laughter and wit. It hasn't been the same around here without you."

A baby's cry interrupted the merriment.

"What on earth is that?" queried Jonathan. "Surely there is not a baby in the Williams house, is there?"

"That's a little surprise we have for you. Your Mother gave birth to twins about six months ago," said Father.

"But there are no twins in the Williams' family, are there?"

"Not until these two."

"You never wrote to me about this utterly surprising event."

"Well, to tell you the truth, we were a little surprised about it ourselves."

Missy could not believe her ears. Her father was lying to Jonathan. Those twins belonged to Abagail and a man she refused to reveal as far as Missy knew. But you would never convince her that the Teacher had been the father of the twins. That was now a mystery she would have to solve by herself.

Chapter 8:
Leaving, Returning and a Meeting

Next morning, donned in her traveling clothes, Abagail came down the stairs. Again, her eyes betrayed the fact she had been crying and really did not want to leave the Williams home where her precious twins would remain. The twins had been allowed to remain in her bedroom the night before and she held each one close and loved them all during the night.

Her blue traveling dress and velvet bonnet matched her beautiful blue eyes. The small boots she wore were made of finest cream-colored leather. The smile she wore did not betray the broken heart in her breast.

The whole Williams family were on hand to wish her "God Speed" and "A Pleasant Journey". Not the least of which was the son Jonathan, who simply could not believe he had not met this beautiful creature before.

As the wagon pulled away, Mother motioned to Jonathan to follow her to the front room of the house. She closed the huge pocket doors and asked him to sit upon the couch with her. She had seen the look in Jonathan's eyes as gazed at Abagail and realized he was very much in love with her.

"Jonathan," she began. "I must tell you that Abagail is actually not our cousin. She was adopted, when she was a baby, by your father's sister and raised by her and her husband. Her parents died in a fire of their home. A neighbor, who was passing by, saw the fire and was able to rescue the baby girl. I thought you should know, since you seem to be so 'taken' with her."

Jonathan responded, "Really? I had no idea. Mother, is this that little skinny, blonde girl named Edwina that I used to play with?"

"One and the same," replied his mother.

"Then, it's alright if I try to court her?"

"I believe so," said his Mother. "However, she has been very ill while staying with us. She had dysentery and several rounds of stomach problems. If I were you, I would want to wait a while to go to her home to visit her."

At this, Jonathan was very sober, "I know how that can make you as weak as a kitten. I've treated those who were suffering from that disease. I will wait at least a month before trying to meet her again."

For the next few months, Jonathan made himself busy following old Doctor McMillan around as he made house calls. Doctor McMillan confessed to Jonathan that he had planned to retire as soon as Jonathan returned from England. He would be glad to hand over the practice to Jonathan because he knew the younger man had been trained in the latest techniques of medicine in England. The two of them became close friends but the good Doctor never revealed the truth about Abagail's stay at the Williams farm.

Time heals a lot of things and after about six months, Abagail told her parents that she would like to visit the William's household again. This time, her mother insisted that she go with her. After all, she didn't want to have Abagail stay as long as before. Besides, her Mother wanted to see the twins that Abagail kept talking about.

They arrived late that night and were welcomed warmly.

"What a surprise. We were wondering how long you would stay away," said Mother Martha. "The twins have grown so much since you were here." Then she turned to her sister-in-law and said, "Come on in and rest. I'll have Agnes bring in some food. You must be hungry after that long journey."

Abagail could hardly contain her happiness at seeing the twins.

"Mother, come quickly. The twins are playing in the living room. You must see them now," called Abagail.

Both children looked as she entered the room. Abagail ran to them and began to hug and kiss them. The little girl pushed her away. The boy started crying and began to crawl toward Mother Martha. At this, Abagail looked bewildered.

Mother Martha said to the unbelieving Abagail, "You must remember, they haven't seen you in such a long time. Give them some time to get used to you again. They are very loving and sweet children." With that spoken, she went to the crying boy child and picked him up. She wiped away his tears and patted his back.

"Charles, this is Abagail. She would like to play with you for a while," said Mother Martha as she handed him to Abagail. This time, he looked up at his real mother and smiled. As soon as the little girl, Charlene, saw him on Abagail's lap, she crawled over and tried to push him off. "No!" she cried, and tried to climb onto the same lap. Her green eyes were livid with jealousy. Abagail reached down and got her with her other hand and sat loving them and talking to them both.

"Charlene, you must not be jealous of your brother. I love you both the same," crooned Abagail.

Her Mother, Elizabeth, teased her, saying, "The way you're carrying on over those babies, one would think they were your own. She laughed at the thought that they could actually belong to Abagail. "Soon you will marry and have children of your own."

Elizabeth could not know how much Abagail wished she could tell the world that she was their Mother. But Mother and Father Williams had helped her with her problem when she needed help so badly. No, she must never reveal the secret.

Jonathan came into the room and watched as Abagail loved the children.

"Hello, Abagail," he greeted her with a smile. "Mother said you were coming for a visit. It's so nice to see you again. The twins have grown and taken on their own personality, haven't they? Charlene is very jealous of any attention shown to Charles. Charles just lets her have her way, even when she takes his toys and won't give them back."

She looked up into the handsome face she had been dreaming about for months.

"Hello yourself," she returned. "I see that you are correct. She wants the attention but I wonder how protective she would be if she saw someone trying to harm him. Aren't they precious? I just couldn't wait to see them again."

After a while, the babies started to yawn and Mother Martha took them up to bed.

"May I help tuck them in," asked Abagail.

"Of course, you may," said Mother Martha. "When you start a family of your own, you will need to know all about babies." No one suspected she said this for the benefit of those who were in the room, but Missy knew.

"Before you go upstairs, I would ask that when you come down, we could go for a ride. I have a gentle horse named Star who would be good for you to ride," Jonathan called after her.

"I would be delighted, but I'm tired tonight," she called back. "How about in the morning?"

"Sounds good to me," said Jonathan.

Next morning, Jonathan and Abagail met at the breakfast table and from there walked to the barn where he saddled the two horses for the anticipated ride - maybe as far as the Cave in The Rock. Cook had prepared a picnic lunch consisting of cold fried chicken, bread, pickles, and muffins for dessert.

"Have you ever been to the Cave in the Rock," he asked after they had ridden over the farm and down by the river.

"No, but I've heard it is really something to see. I was told that Pirates used to take cover inside for shelter overnight. Sometimes they stayed there waiting for travelers on the river, to rob them," she returned.

He asked if she had ever heard of the Tuttle's who ran a tavern in the back of the cave.

"No, I don't guess I have," she replied.

The old tale is told that when a stranger came to their tavern, they would kill them, take their valuables and money and throw the bodies in the river to turn up downstream. Their only son had traveled away from home and was returning. He had grown a full beard and wanted to surprise them. Of course, they didn't recognize him and killed him, also. Not until they had thrown his body into the river and were going through his belongings did they realize they had just killed their only son.

"Oh, how awful!" she said. "I cannot imagine killing one of your children, much less your only son."

As they arrived at the cave, she noticed several bushes of blackberries.

"Oh look, at the bushes of blackberries. We need to pick some for a blackberry pie," she said.

"Oh no, please don't go near those bushes," he said. "See the poison Ivy? I would not want to see the whelps on your pretty hands and face."

"You are the Doctor," she told him.

The cave proved to be quite cool in the back where they chose to have their picnic. Jonathan brought a blanket from his saddlebag. Having been there before, he knew it might be a little bit chilly.

She shivered as he placed the blanket around her shoulders, whether from the chill or from his touch, she didn't know.

It was a large cave, measuring about 30 feet high, 40 feet wide and about 200 feet from front to back where Missy had hidden that infamous night when she saw her teacher ride, at breakneck speed, to save his life.

They talked the afternoon away. He told her about England and his adventures there. About the Queen and how glad America had a President instead of a King or Queen.

Finally, it was time to return home.

"Abagail, I want to see more of you," he said. "I believe I am falling in love with you. I have had this feeling from the moment I laid eyes on you the morning I returned from England. Would it be possible for me to come to visit you at your home?"

"I would like that very much."

After a week, Abigail was filled with sorrow at leaving the twins again, but she had found a greater happiness with Jonathan. Abagail and her Mother departed the Williams farm.

Over the next two years, Jonathan and Abagail were together as much as possible. So, no one was surprised when he proposed and she said agreed. A June wedding was planned at the large church in Pittsburg.

Meanwhile, Missy had met someone.

The family with the church pew directly across from the Williams' pew moved to New York. One Sunday morning, she arrived for church and looked across to find a new family occupying the vacant pew. There was a mother and father and a boy about the age of twelve.

She was thunder struck at the first look at him. He had dark, curly hair that hung on his forehead and a smattering of freckles. His eyes appeared to be hazel in color. As she was gazing in wonder, he caught her staring and she had to turn away.

Her little heart melted. She loved him at first sight. Forget the boyfriend at school, this one would completely rule out anyone else.

He looked over at her with wide eyes and smiled. In fact, he kept looking over at her.

Missy made up her mind that if he looked again, she would wink at him. Sure enough, he peeked at her again and smiled. She winked at him. After this, he did not look back at her again.

"Oh, no," she thought. "He will think I am a hussy."

After church was over, she was embarrassed to look over his way. But when they were outside, he came over to her and said, "You've got a great wink there."

Missy quickly replied, "I just had something in my eye."

"It sure looked like a wink. I'm disappointed that you merely had something in your eye," he said. "My name is Mathew, what's your name?"

"My name is Margaret but everyone calls me Missy," she replied. "I guess we'll be seeing each other at church now"

"I really hope so," he said softly. And with that comment, he joined his parents in their wagon and was gone.

They met at church every Sunday and talked out behind the church. One sunny afternoon, during a church meeting, they held hands and walked out through the cemetery. It was there, he placed the first kiss on her cheek.

"I will love you forever," he said.

"I will love you forever, too," she said back to him.

Chapter 9:
The Wedding of the Season

It was an enormous church - a massive red brick building with a tall steeple that reached to the sky. The great front doors opened to reveal a stunning white interior with pews for each well-to-do family. Within each enclosed pew, which was about six feet by six feet, were chairs and blankets to cover the family during chilly winter weather. Each pew was enclosed by a short wall about three and a half feet tall. The Williams' pew was beautifully decorated with rose-colored velvet cushions laying on carved chairs of mahogany. It was in a very special place near the front of the church. The nearer the front, the more expensive the rent for the year. Their family had attended church there for three generations and had used the church for other weddings and funerals. It was to be the church in which the wedding of Abagail Henning and Doctor Jonathan Williams would be held.

A yearlong courtship began after the first visit to the Cave in The Rock. They decided to become engaged at that Christmastime. No one was surprised and all were elated. A June wedding was planned.

In early May, Abagail's mother, Elizabeth, insisted that her daughter wear her own wedding dress as was tradition in most of the well-to-do families. It was while satin with pearl buttons at the cuffs and down the back of the dress. Thousands of beads and pearls adorned the beautiful gown. There was a six-foot train attached to the back of the gown.

One evening, as she and Jonathan planned the wedding, Abagail approached the subject of the white wedding gown.

"Jonathan, I have a secret to tell you," Abagail began. "When you hear the secret, you may change your mind about marrying me. . . I mean, I love you so much, I can hardly bear to confess this to you but, if you change your mind, I will understand."

With that statement, she burst out crying.

"What on earth could you tell me that could change my mind about marrying you? Please stop crying. I believe our love can withstand anything," he said.

Then he laughed, "Did you murder someone?"

"Don't laugh - I'm very serious."

"Alright let's hear your secret and let me be the judge of whether I still want to marry you, alright?"

"I am not a Virgin," she blurted out. "Now, there it is. My secret is out. I will understand if - - -."

"Oh, my darling sweet one," interrupted Jonathan. "I feel I must confess also. Neither am I a Virgin. This must never come between us."

"Mother wants me to wear her white wedding dress and white is for virgins."

"Wear that white dress and hold your head up high. I'm sure other brides have worn a white dress for their wedding who were not as pure as you are. But I love you even more for being honest and telling me. You are going to be the most beautiful bride ever to walk down that church isle."

So, she wore the dress.

On the day of the wedding, the church was decorated with lovely yellow roses (which were Abagail's favorites), and over 200 people were seated inside the church. The dining hall was also decorated with yellow roses and contained a buffet of food fit for royalty.

The wedding music began, and the preacher, the groom, best man, and other groomsman emerged from behind the alter. The best man and groomsman came from England where they were still in school at Oxford University. Jonathan was elated that they took time out of their studies to do this honor for him.

Next came the maid of honor, Edwina, and Missy, her bridesmaid. Both wore yellow dresses of finest silk with beaded bodices. They wore white shoes. A circle of roses, made of ribbons, adorned their dark hair. Edwina could hardly keep from crying as she made her way down the aisle for she thought of how her own wedding, with the man she loved, would never be.

Missy caught the eye of Mathew as she started down the aisle. He smiled at her and she almost lost her composure. However, she tilted her head upwards and continued down the aisle.

Lastly, right before the Bride's entrance, the twins came in. Charles carried the pillow with the wedding ring and Charlene carried the basket of yellow rose petals. At three and a half, they were darling in their tiny yellow outfits. As they made their way down the aisle, Charlene turned to Charles and exclaimed, "Charles, why are you walking so slow? Here, let me have the pillow," she grabbed the pillow from his hands and started faster down the aisle.

Immediately, Charles started to cry. "My pillow. Give it back," he cried even louder.

When Charlene heard this, she turned and ran back to him.

"Alright, you can have it. Just don't cry. I can't stand it when you cry."

"No, I want to carry the roses now. Let me put out the rose petals!"

"Oh, here!" she said as she exchanged the pillow for the basket of rose petals. "Now hurry up. You're holding up the wedding."

When she realized that everyone was laughing, she turned to them and said, "Do not laugh, I fixed it."

And they continued down the aisle.

As Abagail watched the scene play out, she laughed until she almost wet her pants. Once again, she wished she could claim them for her own.

Abagail was a lovely bride in her mother's white wedding dress. She held her head high as she came down the aisle to meet her groom. He smiled with love at the sight of her and held out his hand to her. Her adopted father, Harry, gave her away.

The wedding vows were traditional and everyone cheered as Jonathan kissed his Bride and they began their journey into what they hoped would be a long and happy marriage.

After the wedding, everyone moseyed into the dining hall.

Missy knew Mathew would be there and she hoped she could meet him at the reception. She sat down two tables away.

As she had hoped, Mathew came to her table. "Hello," he said, "Could I get you some punch?"

Missy answered, "Yes, that would be so nice."

"You looked very pretty when you walked down the aisle a while ago," he said. "I guess I just love you more because you are so pretty."

Missy returned, "Thank you, Matthew, I wanted to look pretty for you today."

"Someday, we'll have a big wedding just like this, Missy, I promise," he declared.

After he had given her the cup of punch, he sat down and began to drink his own cup of punch. "When they cut the cake, I'll get us each a piece, alright?"

She nodded her agreement.

The table for the punch and wedding cake was decorated with a white linen tablecloth with white lace covering the top of the table. The sterling silver punch bowl and dipper had been shined until they glistened. White candles rested in the sterling silver candle holders. Yellow roses lined the length of the table. It was a beautiful sight to behold.

Everyone was seated at the various tables and were very festive, laughing and talking at the same time. It was a wonderful wedding in every sense.

It was time to cut the wedding cake. The bride and groom were behind the table with the sterling silver knife in her hand and his hand on hers. He bent down and whispered to her, "I will love you forever, my beautiful Abagail."

When she looked up she saw, standing before her with the twin, Charles in his arms, was the man who had raped her.

His wife was holding her little girl, Charlene. They were both laughing and talking to the two children. As soon as he recognized her, he turned and began to leave. He said to his wife, "I'll take Charles back to the table. Please bring me a piece of cake, if you can while holding Charlene."

His wife replied, "I cannot hold her and bring two pieces of cake. Wait up and I will sit her in the chair and come back for the cake."

Abagail quickly withdrew her hand and almost cut his in her haste. There had been nowhere to go or hide from him. She almost fainted and stepped back from the table.

"How dare him come to her wedding!!" she thought. "And of all people, for him to have his hands on my babies!! Dear God, please take care of them," she prayed.

As she was looking, Mother Martha went to their table and sat down with them. Then Charles reached for her and she took him from the man's arms.

"That's it, Charles, don't let that man hold you," she thought.

"What's wrong darling?" Jonathan asked her, "Are you alright? You look as if you had seen a ghost."

"I'm alright, it's just a little warm in this place," Abagail said. "Let's cut the first piece of cake so they can serve it to the other people."

His wife came back for the two pieces of cake. "I hope you get to feeling better, Abagail. I was rather queasy on my wedding day, too."

The woman had no idea.

Chapter 10:
New York and a Chance Meeting

After the wedding, Dr. and Mrs. Jonathan Williams settled down in a fine house in the better side of Pittsburg. His practice had grown since taking over from old Doctor McMillan and they were in the full circle of good friends.

Abagail shopped in the best dress shops and had a cleaning lady every Friday. She was very happy with her new life.

They still attended the same church where they were married with a pew almost to the front of the church. Abagail did an extraordinary job of decorating the pew and they were proud to sit there each Sunday.

Time passed and they were ready to start a family. After three years, Abagail found she was pregnant again. Jonathan was extremely pleased and although he was hoping for a boy, he told her he really did not care if it was a boy or a girl, he would be happy if both she and the baby were to be alright.

Jonathan received an invitation to attend a new medical convention in New York and learn the new methods of practice. He was both excited and apprehensive about leaving Abagail in her eighth month of pregnancy. Jonathan asked Missy to come and stay with Abagail while he was gone and she agreed to take care of her.

"Oh, Jonathan, how I wish I could go to New York with you," Abagail said. "Will you bring me a new dress and new boots and parasol?"

"Of course, I will. Only the best for my beautiful wife," he returned.

"I will not always be big and fat like I am now. I will leave the choice of the color up to you. Surprise me! I do love surprises, as you know," she teased.

"I am so torn between leaving you and needing to attend this convention. I know old Dry McMillan will be on standby in case you need him, but I still don't feel right going to New York without you. Maybe next year we can both go to New York and just enjoy the trip. The problem right now is that you could not take riding to that City in the most wonderful carriage I could find. The rough roads would be too much for you in the eighth month of pregnancy. You would surely have a miscarriage. No, we must wait for another year my darling. I promise not to visit a 'Cat House' while I am gone," he teased her.

"Oh, you rogue!" she laughed as she threw a pillow at him. "I never know when you are teasing me and when you are not!"

He turned serious, "I will be concerned about you and the baby the whole time I am gone," he said. "I could never live if something happened to you."

"We will both be alright while you are gone. I promise to eat right and take it easy except for my daily walk as you have told me," she returned.

He wrapped his strong arms around her and held her tenderly, kissing her face and lips.

Four days later, he was on his way to the big city of New York. He was driving the new carriage they had just purchased a month ago. It was quite grand - black with curtains that could be let down in case of rain. The horse was black and was a strong one. Jonathan was in a jaunty mood after he finally got out of town and was really looking forward to being with other doctors who were coming to learn the latest techniques and discoveries in medicine.

It was a three-day trip stopping to overnight at road houses that offered meals and care for the horse. He found the places very accommodating with tasty food and warm beds. The horse was well cared for with water and feed.

Jonathan arrived in New York at two o'clock in the afternoon and checked in at the large hotel in which the convention would be held. It would have been overwhelming had he not seen other large hotels while living in England. The lobby was majestic and demanded admiration for the decorations which adorned the walls. The floors were marble and the woodwork was deeply carved and polished for a look of both dignity and money. Yes, it was quite a hotel.

After he had checked in and saw that the horse had been taken care of, he decided to go for a walk and look around the immediate area before dinner.

As he was strolling, another man appeared to be trying to cross the street when a runaway horse and carriage came careening down the street and hit the man. On down the street, someone stopped the horse and carriage but the damage had been done. The man lay there lifeless, it appeared.

Jonathan rushed out to the man and observed that he was still breathing raggedly. It was apparent his left arm was broken and possibly some ribs also. He was bleeding at the mouth and moaning.

"Can you hear me?" Jonathan asked the man.

"Yes," came the feeble reply.

"I'll get you to the Hospital," Jonathan told the man whose face seemed to look familiar.

Upon arriving at the Hospital in a wagon that Jonathan flagged down, the man was immediately taken to the emergency room where his arm was set and he was examined for other injuries. It was determined that some ribs were broken as Jonathan had suspected.

After the man had been taken to a room, Jonathan visited him.

"Whew, you gave me a scare there for a while," Jonathan said to the man. "You look so much like a young man I used to know back in my home town of Philadelphia, Pennsylvania. What is your name?"

"My name is Theodore Schnell," the man managed to speak out of the corner of his bruised mouth.

"Theodore Schnell? Why that's the reason I thought you looked familiar. I'm Jonathan Williams, your old playmate!" exclaimed Jonathan.

"Well, I will swear! I do not believe this good fortune to meet up with you again. What are you doing in New York? Where are you staying? How did you come to be in the right place at the right time to save me? Can we have lunch and talk over old times?" The man struggled to talk, but was so excited to see his old friend that he was groping for words.

"Whoa, my old friend, I'll answer all your questions when we meet for lunch. I am staying at the Waldorf Astoria which is close to where you were almost killed. I had just gone out for a walk after having arrived in New York. I am here for a doctor's convention at the hotel. How about Dinner tomorrow night at the hotel, say at six-thirty? Then we can talk about old times and what you are doing in New York. For now, you need to rest. If you are not at the hotel tomorrow night, I will visit with you here in the hospital, agree?" asked Jonathan.

"Agreed. I have so much to tell and ask you," said Theodore.

The next day, Jonathan attended the convention and learned new methods of treating influenza, and Louis Pasteur's discovery of bacteria when he examined his spit under a microscope before and after he drank hot coffee. It was a different world he was learning. So many innovative ideas and techniques. The first day was really an eye opener.

As excited as he was over the new medical information he was learning, Jonathan could hardly wait for evening to come to meet with his former play mate.

At precisely six-thirty, Theodore Schnell walked into the dining room of the Waldorf Astoria to meet his old pal Jonathan Williams.

The two men shook hands heartily and it was evident they were looking forward to talking together. They ordered dinner and ate with much relish, except Theodore's mouth was still sore, and he had to eat carefully.

"You first," said Theodore. "What are you doing in New York?"

"You remember that I traveled and stayed in Europe?" Jonathan asked.

"Yes, I remember envying you for getting to go there"

"Well, I studied at Oxford University and then got serious. I began to study medicine and found that I loved the profession - so I became a Doctor", said Jonathan.

"Where do you practice?" asked his friend.

"In Philadelphia and surround areas. We've lived there going on three years," Jonathan told him.

"So, you are married," Theodore asked. "Who did you marry?"

"I married the most beautiful girl in the world, Abagail Henning. She is now eight months pregnant or she would have come with me to this convention.

Theodore almost choked on the bite of steak he was chewing. He managed to swallow it and had to cough several times.

"Are you alright," asked Jonathan.

"Yes, I am quite alright. Must have been a bit of fat in the piece of steak," replied Theodore.

"I was about to hit you on the back then I remembered you have broken ribs," said Jonathan.

"Thank you. I seem to vaguely remember Abagail Henning. Does she have other children?" Theodore queried.

"Oh no, she has never been married," said Jonathan, "except to me."

"How is your sister, Edwina? Did she ever get married? I left so suddenly, she must hate me. However, I must tell you that because a lie was told about me, some men of the county believed the lie and took it upon themselves to rid the county of my presence. What they could not have guessed is that they did me a great favor," said Theodore.

"To answer your question, no, Edwina is not married. She teaches school in the county now and still cries at night for a man who left her there without ever contacting her. Could you be that man?" asked Jonathan.

"I am afraid I am that man. One the of the provisions of the men allowing me to leave the county was that I promise never to contact anyone in the county again. I have kept that promise," replied Theodore. "I would give everything I own to be able to contact her, make things right and marry her. We were to announce our engagement that Christmas. I love her more than life itself but have no way to contact her.

"If what you are saying is true, I will be glad to tell my sister and if she is willing, I can bring her to New York to meet you," declared Jonathan.

"I swear everything I have told you is true. I swear it on my mother's grave. I would be ever so grateful if you would do this for me. As I said previously, the men did me a favor. With the hundred dollars they gave me, I was able to get to New York and meet up with some of my other friends here. They happened to be investing in stocks and bonds and helped me to invest what money I had left after traveling to New York. I am now quite wealthy and can provide for Edwina as I never could have done by teaching school back in the county where we lived.

"Then, it's settled! I will return with or without her in a month or two and contact you. I need your address so I will be able to find you when I return," said Jonathan. "I will be here for three more days then I will return home."

"How I wish I could return with you, but I dare not break my promise to those five men," said Theodore.

"I will see what I can do about that also," said Jonathan.

"No! Please don't mention my name to anyone except Edwina," Theodore said.

"If you say so, I will not. However, I would be willing to try to clear this up with the five men. I do have some influence in the county," said Jonathan.

"Just let sleeping dogs lie for now," said Theodore.

"Alright, I will," said Jonathan.

With that said, they shook hands and looked forward to meeting again in a month.

Chapter 11:
Missy Calls on Fisherman Joe

Missy always enjoyed getting to stay at Abagail and Jonathan's house. This time it was to be different though. She would be responsible for taking care of the expectant Mother

The two of them read and played games of cards and put puzzles together. Sometimes, some of Abagail's friends came over to play cards and have tea with her. Nothing, however, could make her comfortable and her back had to be rubbed after she took the daily walk which Jonathan had told her to take.

Abagail missed Jonathan and sometimes cried because he was gone.

Missy entertained Abagail with stories of the twins, Charlene and Charles, and she never tired of learning about their little antics. Missy told her about how protective Charlene was about Charles. Charlene was jealous if more attention was paid to Charles than to her, but would stand between Charles and the dog that was barking at them. Once, when they were playing around a mud puddle, Charles fell down in the puddle.

Charlene immediately took him to the kitchen and demanded that Agnes the cook clean him up. When Agnes told her, she didn't have time to do that because she was preparing supper, Charlene threatened her by saying, "If you don't stop right now and get him cleaned, I will see that you get fired." Of course, Agnes didn't get fired and little Miss Charlene got to stand in the corner for her punishment."

Missy told her about the time the twins were sick and Charlene told her mother to take care of Charles first because she just could not live if something happened to Charles. They had the flu but survived it because Jonathan took care of them. She made a point of telling Abagail about the twins because Missy knew that Abagail was really the twin's mother.

Jonathan had been gone two days when Abagail began to be in some pain. She decided to abstain from doing the daily walking and laid on the drawing room couch most of the time. Her feet began to be swollen and once again, she had morning sickness.

Missy stayed in a chair beside her and brought her sweet iced tea, read to her and tried to take Abagail's mind from her condition.

Dr. McMillan came by every day to check on Abagail as he had promised Jonathan he would do. On Wednesday, however, he had to tell her that he had death in the family and would be gone three days. He assured Abagail that he felt she would be alright while he was gone and would be to see her as soon as he returned. Although both Abagail and Missy were a little apprehensive, they were in no position to tell the doctor not to go anywhere, especially when there was a death in his family.

So, they watched the doctor leave and Abagail suggested that they have a special prayer for the doctor's journey and that everything would be alright while he was gone. Missy whispered a second prayer for Abagail's swollen feet that the expectant mother did not tell the doctor about.

Two more days passed without incident, but at three o'clock in the morning Abagail woke and screamed out in pain.

Missy jumped up and ran to Abagail's side. "What is wrong?" cried Missy.

"I believe I am having labor pains," replied Abagail. "What will I do if I keep having them? They mean that the baby is going to be born and both Jonathan and Dr. McMillan are gone. I cannot have the baby without a doctor to help me."

Missy thought to herself, "Now, Missy, you cannot panic. There is a solution to every problem." Then she remembered that there was another doctor close by - Fisherman Joe! Somehow, she had to get word to him and get him here to deliver this baby.

"Abagail, I know another doctor but I have to go get him," Missy told her.

"No! Do not leave me. I cannot have this baby without you here!" Abagail almost shouted.

"I will come right back," said Missy. "I have to get someone to stay with you while I go for another doctor"

"What other doctor?" asked Abagail. "You cannot leave me here. There is no other doctor."

"Yes, there is. I just have to convince him to come and deliver the baby," Missy told her.

Missy ran from the room and went next door to Mrs. Dugan and explained the situation.

Mrs. Dugan came at once and went to sit with Abagail while Missy saddled one of the horses and began her long ride out to Fisherman Joe's shack.

She rode as fast as she dared in the dark until she got to the shack and knocked loudly on the door.

Fisherman Joe finally woke and came to the door, surprised to see Missy. "What in the world are you doing out at this time of night," he asked.

"I know I promised to never reveal your secret that you are a doctor, but I am begging you to do this one thing for me." said Missy.

"What is so important that you ask that of me?" asked Fisherman Joe.

"My sister-in-law is about to have a baby and she is only eight months pregnant. Her husband, my brother, is a doctor, but he is out of town to attend a doctor's convention in New

York. The other doctor in town had to leave town for a funeral. There is no one to help her. Please come and deliver the baby. No one else knows you are a doctor and you could save both her and the baby. Please, I am begging you to do this," she cried. By this time, she was crying so hard, she could hardly speak.

"Only for you will I come and deliver the baby," he said quietly. "Let me get my horse saddled up."

They rode at as fast pace as they dared in the dark and reached Abagail's house in record time.

They could hear Abagail moaning as they ran through the front door.

As they entered the bedroom where Abagail lay, she shouted at Missy, "Where have you been? Mrs. Dugan could not stay any longer and left me alone by myself. I have been so scared that you would not come back. I need a clean cloth to bite down on. Who is that with you? Is he the doctor you went to get?"

"Here is a clean cloth to bite on. Yes, this is doctor Joe. He has been a doctor for many years but I will tell you all about him after we get this baby delivered," Missy told her.

Doctor Joe began to talk to Abagail. "Now relax, if you can. How many months are you along?" he asked.

"I believe about eight, but I could be off a bit," Abagail answered.

Doctor Joe turned to Missy. "Get some hot water for me as quickly as you can. Where can I wash my hands?" he asked.

"Over there in the corner is the wash bowl. I will get the hot water as fast as I can," Missy told him.

In about fifteen minutes Missy returned with a kettle of hot water, wash cloths and towels. "Is there anything I can do to help?" she asked.

"When the time comes, you can be a lot of help. Have you ever seen a baby born?" Doctor Joe asked.

"No, but I did watch a baby calf being born once," she answered.

The doctor chuckled, "Well, this is similar, but not the same."

During the next few hours Abagail slept and woke to the pain of childbirth. At eleven fifteen in the morning, the baby was born.

He was a small baby boy and he cried as soon as the doctor slapped him on the butt.

Abagail lay back on the pillows for a minute then asked, "Is it a boy?"

"He is a fine healthy boy. Now, he is a little smaller than usual because he came into the world a little bit early, but he is breathing well and has all ten fingers and ten toes," the doctor told her.

"Thank you so much doctor," Abagail whispered. "My husband will be so happy to know there is another doctor in town."

"I am not practicing as a doctor right now," he said. "I have been through a very difficult time in my life, lost my whole family in a hotel fire in New York and almost lost control of myself. Missy here and a little boy named Jake are the only other people who know I am a doctor. I need you to keep my secret for a while longer until I can gain control of my life again. Can you do that?" he asked.

Abagail was at once thankful and pitying the doctor. "Of course, I will keep your secret for as long as you want me to."

"I must be going now. The fish may be biting and I make my living by selling fish right now. I will be back to check on both you and the baby each day until your husband returns," Doctor Joe told her. "I will come and go by the back door and bring fish so no one will suspect the real reason for my visit."

After he had gone, Abagail demanded that Missy tell her how she came to know he was a doctor.

"It is a long story," Missy began. First, she swore Abagail to secrecy then she told Abagail all about the time some men at the cave who accused a young man of something he did not do and made him leave the county. She did not tell any names and said she did not know the men. She crossed her fingers behind her back so God would forgive her telling a lie. Then she related the visit to the cave, in the night and how they threw a man into the river and Fisherman Joe rescued him. She told how he fixed the man's broken arm and sewed up the cut on the man's face. After that, Fisherman Joe admitted he was a doctor to her. She also told Abagail about her father's and some of the neighboring farmers' visit to the men and some of the men left town.

"Who were the men?" Abagail asked.

I did not recognize any of them," Missy lied again with her fingers crossed.

Doctor Joe came every day as he promised until Dr. McMillan returned from the funeral of his relative. Missy met him at the back door and warned him that the other doctor was with Abagail.

"Well, well, Missy sure did an excellent job of delivering that baby. I will have to get her for a nurse if I ever get caught like this again," Missy heard the doctor say.

"Yes, a doctor could not have done better than Missy," Abagail told him.

Missy stayed in the kitchen until the doctor left then went into Abagail's bedroom. "Did you just tell Dr. McMillan that I delivered the baby?" she asked.

"I was caught and had to tell him something. I promised to keep Fisherman Joe's secret. What else could I do? You are now a heroine," Abagail laughed.

"I hope no one else asks me to deliver a baby. I am not even going to try," Missy laughed with her.

When the baby boy was a week old, Jonathan came home. He was both elated and astounded.

"I cannot believe the baby came early. But most of all, I cannot believe that Missy delivered our baby boy," Jonathan said.

They named the baby Jonathan Edward Williams and he was christened the following Sunday.

Chapter 12:
The Judges Wife and the Twins

Jonathan and Abagail had come to the farm for dinner and of course, Abagail was playing with the four-year-old twins and holding the new baby.

"Why doesn't he have more hair?" asked Charlene.

"Because he is not very old and he was born without a lot of hair. Most babies do not have any hair. His hair will grow out as he gets older," said Abagail to her daughter.

"I really like the baby," said Charlene. Charles nodded his head in agreement with his sister. "Me too," he said. They played with the baby and had a very good time hugging and sitting with Abagail.

At thirteen, Missy still liked to read in her favorite spot behind the couch in the library and she was there when Jonathan ushered Edwina into the room.

"Have I got news for you, Edwina," Jonathan almost shouted. "You will never guess who I ran across while I was in New York at the doctor's convention."

"I cannot even try to guess. Who was it?" Edwina asked.

"Your old boyfriend, Theodore Schnell," said Jonathan.

"Do not even mention his name to me!" Edwina said in a terse voice. "He left and did not tell me or write or try to contact me! I do not want to hear anything you must say about meeting with that... that... Oh, I do not know what to call him. I hate him!"

"No, you have it all wrong, Edwina," said Jonathan. "He was forced to leave here with only the clothes on his back and one hundred dollars. He was given an ultimatum that he never contacts anyone here under penalty of death. He wanted to contact you, but could not do it."

"Why would anyone want to do this to him? He was a very good teacher and I believe everyone respected him," Edwina replied.

"He said someone told a lie on him and some of the men of the town believed the lie. He would not tell me what the lie was, just that it was bad enough for them to threaten him with killing him," Jonathan told her. "He said he loves you more than life itself and he wishes you to come to New York and marry him. He met with some of his former friends in New York and they helped him make some very profitable investments in the stock market much to his advantage." He is a very wealthy man now.

"And you believed him?" Edwina asked.

"He swore on his mother's grave. That is a pretty serious oath," said Jonathan.

"I cannot think of any reason why you would come to me and relate your chance meeting with him. I believe you. You have just made me the happiest woman in the world. Do you know that?" Edwina cried.

"I promised him that I would return to meet him in a month or month and a half - depending on how Abagail is feeling - and I would talk to you and bring you with me if you wanted to meet with him," Jonathan told her.

"Can we start tomorrow? Oh, no, I have to have time to get ready, buy my wedding dress, and other clothing for after the wedding," Edwina said excitedly.

They exited the room with Edwina's laughter ringing throughout the house. She was almost wild in her happiness.

Missy, who had heard the entire conversation, was so happy for her sister. However, she wondered what was going to happen when Abagail met Theodore Schnell and faced him. It was she who had told the lie which caused all the problem. She wondered if Mr. Schnell would confront her or would forgive her.

There was a problem, though - to take or not to take the twins. They would not like being still for the long journey, would be restless and cranky.

During the past four years, the Judge Amos Chandler and his wife Mary Lee had been regular visitors to the Williams farm. The twins grew to love them and the Judge and his wife adored them. After the Judge decided to retire, the twins were a lot of company for them. In fact, the twins could remain at the Judge's home for an entire day at a time. The Judge's wife was overjoyed when Mother Martha asked if they would care to take care of them while the family made the journey to New York for the wedding.

The Judge paled when Missy's father told him who Edwina would be marrying. "My wife and I would like to give them a two-hundred-dollar wedding gift if you will take it to them," the Judge told him.

"I appreciate the gift very much. I will see if Edwina will accept such a large gift. It seems that Mr. Schnell is quite wealthy now. He has made a fortune with the money he was given when he left town," Missy's father told the Judge.

"Then I wish them well," the Judge replied.

"If anything should happen to the twins while we are gone, I will hold you personally responsible," said Missy's father.

"I swear that nothing will happen to either of them while they are in our care and you are gone," declared the Judge.

After one and a half months, the Williams family departed on the long journey to New York City.

The twins waved goodbye to them and rushed into the special room at the Judge's home. Great care had gone into creating a play-room for them. Large rocky horses for both were there plus all kinds of books, a wooden train for Charles and a doll-house with furniture, and several dolls for Charlene.

Charlene played with the doll house and dolls for a while then climbed onto her rocky horse. "I like this horse, but I will be glad when I can ride a real horse," she said.

The Judge's wife, Mary Lee, heard this and told Charlene, "As soon as your father lets us know, we will buy a real horse for you to ride, but for now, you will have to be satisfied with a wooden horse to ride."

Charlene stamped her foot. "I want a real horse now!" she shouted.

The Judge heard her shout and came into the room. "Now Charlene, you must be patient. Now is not the time for a real horse for you. Your father gave us the responsibility of taking care of you and you might get hurt while they are gone. I will not tolerate your shouting at Mary Lee."

At this time, Charles ran over to his sister and said, "Charlene, you must obey what they say. Mother and Father are gone. They might not feed us or take us out in the woods and leave us like Hansel and Gretel. And we would have to find the house made of candy and the witch might get us," He was barely whispering the last part.

"Oh, my dears," said Mary Lee, we would never do that to you both. We love you so much."

Charlene looked at her brother. "You are right. We must obey them until our mother and father get back from New York," she said. Then she turned to the Judge and Mary Lee, "I am sorry and I promise not to have a tantrum again. You have always been kind to us. Maybe someday I will have a real horse, but for now, I will be content with a rocking horse. It is very beautiful."

She surprised the Judge by running to him and climbing onto his lap. She threw her arms around his neck and kissed him on the cheek. Then she slid down from his lap and ran to Mary Lee, and hugged and kissed her on the cheek.

"Will you both forgive me?" she asked.

Both the Judge and Mary Lee smiled and said they forgave her.

"I have a special treat for us all," said Mary Lee. "I made some cupcakes and they are waiting for a certain little boy and girl to eat!"

"Oh, yes, I love cupcakes," cried Charles.

They were very delicious. The children ate two each and drank a small glass of milk. The Judge and Mary Lee had coffee with their cupcakes.

By this time, it was getting late and the twins were tired and wanted to go to bed. One of the bedrooms had been furnished with two little beds, just right for two sleepy children. It did not take long for them to go to sleep after Mary Lee tucked them in and gave them a kiss on the cheek. "I love you both," she said.

The next morning, they awoke to sounds in the back yard.

Charlene sat up in bed and said, "Charles, that sounds like a horse! Come on, get up and let's see what is going on."

They made their way quickly, still in their pajamas, to the back door where they could see that there was really a horse in the back yard. Only, it was a smaller version of a horse. It was a pony with a saddle on its back. It was grey with a white mane and black eyes. The Judge was leading the pony around the back fence and talking to the animal.

"Now, Charity, calm down. The children will be up soon and I want them to like you," he said

Charlene flung the back-door open and ran to the fence.

"It is a horse, it is a horse," she shouted. "I love it already! When can I ride the horse?"

Mary Lee came running out the back door and put her arms around the excited child. "You will have to wait until after breakfast and you have proper clothes on to ride the pony," she said.

The two children returned to the house, put their clothes on and had a breakfast of oatmeal, toast and milk.

As soon as the morning meal was over, they returned to the backyard fence and watched the little pony walk around the fence. Finally, the pony came up to where they were standing. She poked her nose to the fence as if to say, "Who are you two?"

Charles jumped back and exclaimed, "She's going to bite me!"

Charlene tried to calm her brother down by saying "She just wants to get to know us better, Charles. Put your hand out and let her see that you like her."

"But I am afraid of her," said the frightened Charles.

The Judge came out of the house and asked, "Now who wants to ride Charity first?"

"I think I better go first," said Charlene. "Charles is afraid of her."

"Alright Charlene, you go first. That way Charles will see how much fun it will be to ride Charity," said the Judge.

Mary Lee came out of the house and put her arms around the shivering child. "Now Charles, you do not have to ride the pony if you do not want to," she said.

Charles looked up at her and said, "I want to ride the pony, but I just have to get used to riding a real horse instead of a wooden one. I am sure it will be a lot different, won't it?"

After Charlene had ridden seven rounds around the fence, she stopped and dismounted.

"It is your turn, Charles, to ride the pony," she said.

Charles reluctantly walked through the gate and went up to the pony. Charity waited for him to pet her and get acquainted. She stood still while Charles climbed into the saddle and then she began walking around the fence as she had done with Charlene. Suddenly Charles became frightened and screamed. When Charity heard the scream, she was startled and reared up on her hind legs. This threw Charles to the ground.

The Judge, Mary Lee and Charlene all ran to where Charles lay, white faced and moaning that his arm hurt. The Judge picked up the child and took him into the house. It was apparent, from the way the right arm was laying, that it was broken.

Mary Lee said, "Run and get the Doctor. His arm is broken and it must be set right away."

The Judge replied," I will have to get old Dr. McMillan. Doctor Williams has gone to New York for his sister's wedding."

Within thirty minutes, Dr. McMillan came and set the tiny arm in a splint. "Keep him as quiet as you can for the next few days," the doctor told them. "I will check on him every day until Dr. Williams returns." He gave them some medicine to ease the pain and make him sleep.

After the doctor left, Mary Lee began crying. "They trusted us to take care of Charles and Charlene and look what has happened."

Charlene ran to her. "It was all my fault. I never should have asked for a real live horse. Please stop crying. Charles will be alright. I will take care of him and nurse him back to being alright."

After another week, the Williams family returned home without their beloved Edwina and took the twins back home. However, they decided to leave the pony at the Judge and Mary Lee's home for the time being. Mother Martha told the Judge that the twins could ride Charity when they were at their home, in the future.

The Judge and Mary Lee were happy when Mother Martha said this because they looked forward to the twin's visit so much.

Chapter 13:
Trouble in New York

Everyone was in high spirits on the morning of their departure for New York City. Edwina had purchased several items of clothing to take on her honeymoon and planned to buy some more items when they arrived in New York.

Missy was excited to be a bridesmaid again and the thought of being in the big city was exhilarating to say the least. She hated it that she would miss seeing Matthew, but she would be back in a week and a half so it would be alright for her to go.

Jonathan said he would be glad to see his old school buddy and happy to see his sister so vibrant and lovely as all brides-to-be usually are.

Abagail, however, was dreading to meet the groom because of the lie she had told about him, causing him to be run out of the county. She hoped that no one, but the sheriff and the men he took with him knew who she had named as the man who had raped her. The sheriff had assured her, afterwards, that the men of the county had taken care of the situation and the young teacher would not bother her again. If it was going to be a good relationship in the family, she must speak with him alone. If that were possible, she had another lie to tell him. She would apologize, ask his forgiveness, beg him not to tell Jonathan, and tell him that she had a miscarriage.

Mother and Father Williams were the only ones who were rather somber because they would be leaving their daughter in New York and would not be able to see her as often as they would like after the wedding.

The almost three-day trip would be long, but their carriages were comfortable and the excitement made the trip enjoyable.

The Waldorf Astoria Hotel was breath taking. Their rooms were extremely beautiful and made the day even more exciting. It was close to dinner time and they dined in the luxurious dining room.

Edwina, Mother, Abagail and Missy decided to go shopping the next day and purchase the rest of Edwina's wedding and honeymoon garments. But before the shopping, they were to go to Theodore Schnell's home to meet with him.

When they arrived at the large home of Theodore Schnell, he greeted them himself at the door and invited them all into the beautiful living room. He immediately went to Edwina and hugged her.

"It is so wonderful to see you," said Theodore. "I prayed so hard that you would come back with Jonathan and marry me."

"Wild horses could not have dragged me from here," Edwina said. "However, I would like to see you alone and talk about the wedding. Am I to understand that you have arranged everything for the wedding?" she asked.

"Yes, my darling, everything is arranged for us to be married at the St. Paul's Cathedral the day after tomorrow," said Theodore.

They were unaware of anyone else in the room until father coughed. Then they took their eyes off each other and looked at the other people in the room. First Theodore shook hands with the father and mother of the bride, then with Missy. Next, he shook hands with Jonathan. When he saw Abagail, he asked, "So this is the lovely young lady you have told me about, Jonathan?" (Although he had been accused of raping her, he had never seen her.)

Jonathan replied, "Yes, this is my lovely wife. We now have a bouncing baby boy since I last saw you."

Abagail said, "So nice to finally meet you. I have heard so much about you from Jonathan. Oh, the stories he has told me about your escapades when you two were in school. I would like very much to speak with you about some of them when you have a moment to spare."

"And, I would like very much to tell you about them and to ask you about some of your own experiences at your school," he replied.

After the initial meeting at Theodore's home, the women were driven to downtown New York where they shopped in some of the most expensive stores they had ever seen. There were very few 'sales' garments to be found, but they were too excited to be worried about the money they were spending. After all, it was not every day that a daughter got married in New York's St. Paul's Cathedral!

That evening they all met at an Italian restaurant and had a very good evening together.

Before the dessert, Theodore looked over at Abagail and said, "Abagail, I have a funny story I should like to tell you, but I do not want to tell it here. Jonathan knows the story well, so he will not care if I share it with you. Come with me to the side yard." To the others he said, "Excuse us for a moment, please."

Abagail rose and followed him to the side yard

When they were out of earshot of the others, Abagail began her story. As she had rehearsed, she said, "Oh, Theodore, I am so sorry that I have caused you so much trouble and grief. I could not think of another man who was single in the county to accuse of the rape. It was a man who threatened to kill me if I revealed who did it. As it happened, I had a miscarriage, so there is no baby. Again, I am so very sorry. Can you find it in your heart to forgive me? It would cause my marriage to Jonathan to be over if he knew, I am afraid. Please, I am begging you to keep this secret."

"How can I refuse to keep the secret?" he asked. "I cannot ruin my friend Jonathan's marriage and have a good marriage with his sister. I wish I knew the man who did this to you. I would see that he is punished. You have my word that I will not reveal your secret. Actually, you did me a favor. If I had stayed in the county as a school teacher, I would not have had a chance to become the wealthy man I am today. My only regret is the grief it caused to Edwina. I really wondered if she would want to marry me after the prolonged period of time. I did not contact her. Well...I guess we had better go back to the others. Now laugh as if I had told you a funny joke and we will say 'it was a funny story', alright?" he asked.

"I can never thank you enough. You are a true gentleman," she said. She turned back into the room and began laughing as if she had heard the funniest of stories. Theodore followed her with a smile from ear to ear.

"It must have been a really funny story," declared Jonathan.

"You would never believe it," retorted Theodore, as he took his seat beside Edwina.

The dessert was so very, very delicious and the rest of the evening ha much laughter and fun. Then it was time for goodbye except for Theodore and Edwina who had a lot to talk about after an absence of almost four years. They lingered over cups of over cups of hot coffee that had come with the dessert and talked.

"Now," said Edwina, "will you tell me why you left Lancaster county without saying goodbye and why you have not contacted me for four years."

"I will start from the beginning and tell you all about that terrible night when I was forced to leave without telling anyone. Five men came to my house and called me out into the yard. They tied my hands, put me on a horse and took me to the cave in the rock down by the river. Do you remember the cave?" he asked.

Edwina nodded her head that she remembered.

"When we arrived at the cave, they untied my hands and told that a rumor had been told that I had done a terrible deed. I tried to deny the lie but they would not believe me. Finally, one of the men, who seemed to be the leader, gave me one hundred dollars and advised me that if I did not leave they would kill me. I was not to go home, not to contact anyone that night and never to come back to the county," he told her.

"It must have been something awful that they accused you of doing. What was it?" she asked.

It is better that I not reveal the thing they accused me of doing," he told her. "Actually, they did me a favor as you will see when I finish my story. I did not stop riding until I could tell the horse was beginning to be too tired. I slept in a farmer's barn that night and paid him for feed for the horse next morning. He invited me in for breakfast and then I continued my way. I traveled for another day and a half and came to New York. One of my old school chums had told me that if I ever came to New York, to look him up. I looked him up and he helped me to get established and make money in the stock market. Being familiar with figures from working as a school teacher, I caught on quickly and have made a very good living here in New York. I did not see anyone from back home until Jonathan came to town so there was no way to contact you. I love you, always have and always will. If you will forgive me and marry me, you will make me the happiest man alive."

"Yes, I will marry you. I came to New York to marry you and did not hesitate. I love you as much as you love me," she declared.

When he took her back to the hotel, he said, "Soon we will not ever have to be parted again," and kissed her good night.

The next day Theodore and Edwina toured the City of New York and made final arrangements for the wedding. She was so happy to be with her beloved and he was enjoyed having her by his side and loving her.

The wedding next day was very solemn and beautiful. The huge Cathedral echoed their wedding vows. It was decorated with white lilies and her wedding bouquet was made of white lilies and daisies with long white ribbon streamers. Her dress of white was covered with French lace and had lovely pearl buttons down the back and at the wrists. Her veil of French lace cascaded to the floor to the edge of the six-foot train behind the dress. The bridesmaids wore pink dresses and carried bouquets of daisies. Jonathan was best man and another friend of the groom was the other groomsman.

Several of Theodore's friends attended the wedding that day. The wedding reception was in a large building across the street from the church. It was catered with exquisite food. The wedding cake was four tiered and a tiny bride and groom adorned the top layer. A small orchestra played music for the reception and everyone danced until one o'clock in the morning.

Theodore and Edwina retired to their home and left for their honeymoon in England the next day. The white carriage that picked them up for the journey to the ship was adorned with flowers. The horse had a ring of flowers around his neck and the driver had flowers around his top hat. There was a sign on the back of the carriage that read, "Just Married".

A happier couple could not be found that day.

Chapter 14:
Heartbreak and Happiness

The long journey home took a toll on everyone's stamina. They were all tired. There had been tearful goodbyes from father, mother and Missy but the look of happiness on Edward's face quickly dried any tears in their eyes. After all, did they not want Edwina to be happy? Of course, they did!

Since the next day was Sunday, Missy looked forward to seeing Mathew again. It was so wonderful to see him sitting in the pew next to hers and to meet him and get a quick hug after church.

Mother stayed at home with Charles because he was not feeling good and begged to not go to church this Sunday.

Charlene liked to sit with Mathew's mother sometimes and on this Sunday, she asked if she could go over to their pew.

Father granted permission for her to go and set there and Charlene hurried over and climbed on Elizabeth's lap where she usually sat.

"You know that Mathew and Missy love each other, don't you?" Charlene whispered in Elizabeth's ear.

"Do you really think so?" whispered back Mathew's mother.

"Oh, yes," whispered Charlene. "They are going to get married. I heard them say so. And if you will not let them get married, they are going to run away and get married."

Mathew's mother had a stern look on her face after that bit of information.

After church, Missy asked Charlene what she and Mathew's mother had been whispering about.

"Oh, I just told her what I heard you and Mathew talking about. How you two were going to run away and get married," Charlene told her.

"Charlene! How could you do such a thing?" Missy asked.

"Well, you did say that, didn't you? Did I do something wrong?" Charlene began to cry.

"Do not cry. It is too late, the damage has been done," said Missy.

During all the next week, Missy could not shake a feeling that something was about to go wrong.

The next Sunday, her fears were confirmed for Matthew was not in the pew with his mother and father. In fact, the pew was empty. No one knew where that family had gone for the day.

Missy dreaded to go to church the following Sunday. When she looked over to Mathew's pew, his mother and father were there without Mathew. This time, Charlene was not allowed to go and sit on Elizabeth's lap.

After church, Missy gathered her courage and went to Mathew's mother to ask where he was.

"We thought things were going a little too fast between you and Matthew. He is now in an academy away from here," his mother told her.

"Will you give me his address so I can write to him?" asked Missy.

"We do not think that would be wise," Matthew's mother said. "I told him to put any letters to you in with my letters and I would give them to you." She turned and walked away from Missy.

Tears streamed down Missy's young face for she knew she would not receive any letter that came into Matthew's mother's hand.

No one else knew where Matthew had been sent, so Missy had no choice but to wait and see when Matthew would come home.

Over the next year, some Sundays Mathew's parents would be absent from church and Missy could only guess that they had gone to see Mathew. She did not ever get a letter from him. Now it was her turn to cry for someone she loved. Now she knew how despondent Edwina must have felt during the time she did not hear from Theodore.

Finally, after two years, she went to a dance with Dan Scherer. He was a very nice boy who had asked to date her during the time she and Mathew were dating.

"I guess you have given up on Mathew's ever coming back to you, haven't you?" he asked.

"I guess so," Missy answered back.

"I am sorry you had to have your heart broken before you would date me, but I guess I am also glad," he stated. "I like you a lot."

"You are a very nice boy and I am glad you waited for me to get over Mathew," she told him. But in her heart, she knew she was not over Mathew and never would get over being in love with Mathew.

Missy decided not to go out with Dan again because she did not want to give him the impression that she liked him that much. So, when he asked her out, she had a previous thing to do or go to or did not feel well. He soon got the message that she was just putting him off.

Missy's parents noticed a change in her. She no longer wanted to go to church on Sunday because of a headache or her stomach hurt or some other flimsy excuse. They guessed the reason, but could do nothing about it. Mathew's parents were not friendly anymore and almost refused to speak on Sunday.

One night, about midnight, something hit Missy's window. She thought it was a limb and ignored it. Then another something hit her window and another and another. She decided to see what it was and as she looked out into the moonlight, she saw Mathew ready to toss another thing at her window. He motioned for her to come down to him.

She threw on some clothes and tiptoed down the stairs and out the front door.

He was waiting and enveloped her in his strong waiting arms. He kissed her waiting lips over and over and held her close to him.

"How many times have I dreamed of doing that," he whispered against her hair. "I love you so much."

"What are you doing here?" she asked.

"Let us get away from the house and go where we can talk," Matthew said.

"I know the perfect place," said Missy. "It is not far from here." She led him to the cave by the river.

"I have a lot to tell you," he said. "When Charlene told my mother that we were planning to run away and get married, my father had a fit. He and my mother took me to an academy for boys and left me. It is very strict and I was not allowed to leave the grounds. My parents came to see me but would not let me come home for fear I would come to see you. I put letters to you in with my parent's mail, but when I did not hear from you, I realized they were not giving my letters to you.

Mother told me that you had married Dan Scherer and I nearly died just thinking about you in his arms. Then another boy's girlfriend wrote and told him that you did not get married to Dan. That was one of the happiest days of my life."

"I did go out with Dan one time, but I could not stand to look at him, so that was all that went on between him and me," she admitted. "I thought you were gone for good."

"I could never forget you. I love you so much," he declared again. "Back at my military school, there is a lot of talk about some of the southern states wanting to form another country. President Abraham Lincoln has sworn that he will not let that happen. It could mean that I and all the others at the academy will be asked to join the Union Army and go into battle against the southern soldiers.

The first battle was at Fort Sumpter on April 12, 1861. It looks like we are headed into a full scale civil war. If we are called to go into battle, I want to have the memory of marrying you."

"My parents think I am on a field trip for the academy. The boys back at the academy are covering for me until I return. I have found a preacher who will marry us. Of course, we will have to keep it a secret until I graduate or go into war. I will give you my address so we can keep in touch. I do not know how else to be sure we can be together in the future, do you? Now, I am asking you if you will go with me and get married tonight?" he asked.

"Yes, I will marry you tonight," Missy answered. "But I will need to return home before daylight if we are to keep our marriage a secret."

"Then we need to go as we are dressed and wake up the preacher. We are wasting time talking about it," Matthew said.

They rode double on his horse until they came to the preacher's house. There they knocked on his door until he awoke and came to the door. He was sleepy eyed and yawning.

"What are you two young people doing out at this time of night?" he inquired. Then he recognized Matthew. "Oh yes, you are the young man who came and asked if I would marry you and your sweetheart," the preacher said.

"Yes sir, I am the one, and this is my bride-to-be," replied Matthew.

"How old are you both?" the preacher asked Mathew.

"I am nineteen and she is seventeen," said Mathew.

"Do your parents know you two are getting married?" the preacher asked Missy.

"No, and we will have to keep it a secret because his parents do not want us to get married. Mathew may have to go to war and we want to be married before anything happens like that, Missy replied. "My parents will be happy because they have seen how heartbroken I have been when I was not allowed to contact Mathew."

"Then come on in and let us get you two married. I know both your parents. I also know that you were going together for some time. I promise you that I will keep your marriage a secret. We will need a witness, so let me get my wife out of bed," said the preacher.

And so, they were married at midnight by preached Ivan Wilkins on May 15, 1861.

They spent their wedding night under the stars on a blanket he had brought for her warmth.

At five o'clock, Mathew told her they needed to get her back to her home before someone missed her.

After they exchanged addresses, Mathew kissed her goodbye and rode off into the darkness.

Chapter 15:
Going to War

News of the beginning of the war between the states reached the citizens of Philadelphia quickly. Men of all ages began volunteering and leaving to join the Union troops. Rallies were held and the women gathered material and sheets to tear and roll for medical bandages.

Dr. Jonathan Williams was among the men who wanted to volunteer. However, with the death of old Dr. McMillan, he did not feel he should leave the town without a doctor.

Abagail, who now had another child, a daughter named Angela, hoped and prayed that her husband would not leave her with the two young children.

At Jonathan's parents' home, where he and Abagail had gone for dinner, he told them of his frustration and how much he wanted to join the Union forces.

Missy listened to him and made the decision to break a promise. After dinner, she motioned to Jonathan to follow her outside.

"I know another doctor here close to where we are standing right now. I promised him to never reveal his secret, but I feel this is a desperate situation and desperate situations call for desperate measures," said Missy.

"Where on earth is there another doctor near here," asked Jonathan.

"Do you know the man we all call Fisherman Joe?" asked Missy.

"Jonathan laughed. "Sure, everyone knows Fisherman Joe. Now do not tell me that he is a doctor," said Jonathan.

"That is exactly what I am telling you. I have seen him set a broken arm and then stitch up a man's face. He made me swear not to tell anyone. He also delivered your son while you were gone to New York. Abagail will vouch for that. She was also sworn to secrecy. We lied about my delivering your son. If you do not believe me, ask Abagail," said Missy.

"I believe you. Can we go and visit him right now?" asked Jonathan excitedly.

"Yes, but I think we need to let the rest of the family know where we are going," advised Missy. "It is not fair to leave them worrying about our taking off without telling them," said Missy.

"Of course, you are right, Missy," said Jonathan.

As the two of them entered the house again, Jonathan told them that he and Missy were going to find another doctor.

At once, Abagail looked at Missy and exclaimed "You have broken a promise, Missy. I know who you are going to visit."

"Desperate situations call for desperate measures," said Jonathan.

He and Missy walked to Fisherman Joe's shack and knocked on the door.

Fisherman Joe opened the door and exclaimed, "To what do I owe the honor of the two of you?"

"Fisherman Joe, there is a terrible need for doctors at the front lines in the war. My brother Jonathan wants so much to volunteer and go and serve with the Union army. He cannot go because it would leave the city without a doctor. I have broken my promise to you and for that I am sorry but you are the only one who can fill the place of my brother," said Missy.

Jonathan asked, "If you are a doctor, what is your full name?"

Fisherman Joe looked at the two-people standing and needing help so badly and made a momentous decision.

"My full name is Joseph Albert Gohagen. I was a doctor for a long time but stopped practicing when my family perished in the hotel fire in New Year. I almost lost my mind for a while. Then I ended up here where it is peaceful and just began a new life," said Joe.

"Joseph Albert Gohagen? You are the famous doctor from Germany whom I studied about in England. Man, why are you not still in the medical world? You have made so many medical discoveries, I doubt I could count them all. Please allow me to shake the hand of a world-famous doctor. I cannot believe I am actually standing in your presence," said Jonathan reverently.

"I am humbled by your speech. I must admit that I have missed the medical world and was seriously considering going back into practice but did not know where to start again," said Doctor Joseph. He held out his hand to Jonathan who shook it with gusto, "I will be glad to begin my medical practice here while you are away. After you return, I will return to Germany and resume my work there again," said Dr. Gohagen.

"I plan to leave within the week. Would you be able to start when I leave? You can just take over my practice and use my office until my return," said Jonathan.

"I will be there in the morning to go over your list of clients, get acquainted with your office and learn what you want me to do," answered Dr. Gohagen.

"I shall see you in the morning then," said Jonathan.

Jonathan and Missy walked back to their parents' home. On the way back, Missy told the whole story about Dr. Gohagen except she left out the part about naming Abagail as the girl who was raped.

When they arrived back at the house, Jonathan sat down in the living room and became very somber.

"I have found a doctor to replace me while I am serving in the Union army. I plan to leave no later than three days from now. I trust you all will see after Abagail while I am away. I am hoping that you, Missy, will see your way to visit with Abagail very, very often and perhaps stay the night with her. Dr. Gohagen has promised to see after her also. I would admonish you three women to keep making bandages for the army. They will be greatly needed. I will write to you when I can and let you know how things are going with me. Please pray that God will go with me and help me to help the men who are wounded and giving their lives for their country," said Jonathan. He stood up and wrapped his arms around his wife and children. They left quietly.

Abagail was able to hold back the tears until they were on their way home in the carriage. Then the flood of tears began. "I guess I knew you would find a way to join the army but I was praying you would not be able to go. I will miss you and worry about you being cold and hungry," she said.

Back at the farm house, Charles stood up and announced that he would be going to join the army also.

"I feel I could shoot as well as any of the soldiers and they need all the men that can carry a gun and fight the Johnny Rebels. I hear they do not want to give up their slaves and set them free. President Lincoln has issued an order that all men must be free and I believe that, too," Charles said.

Mother exclaimed, "But you are only fifteen years old!"

"You cannot go and leave me, Charles, what would I do?" asked Charlene.

"Oh, alright, I will not go right now, but I really feel it is my duty to help win this war," said Charles.

Father sat very still for a long time and was in deep thought, but did not say a word.

Jonathan left on a sunny Wednesday morning. All the family was there at his and Abagail's home to bid him goodbye. The Preacher, Ivan Wilkins led the family in prayer for Jonathan's safety. There were tears and smiles through tears as Dr. Williams rode away.

Missy continued to receive letters from her beloved Mathew and he managed to slip away to visit her as often as he could. Then came the visit when he told her that his class of young men had been volunteered to join the army.

"No! you cannot go! If anything should happen to you, I would not want to live," Missy cried.

That night, they stayed too long in the barn loft where they spent most of their nights together. When they returned to the house, Missy's father was waiting at the front door.

"Where have you two been all night?" he asked.

Mathew spoke first, "Mr. Williams, as you know, my parents did not want us to go together, but we love each other and we have been married for about three months. I am asking first, for your blessing, and second for your secrecy from my parents. I will be going to join the army the day after tomorrow and Missy and I would like to spend this day together before I leave."

"Why am I not surprised?" said Missy's Father. "You have my blessing and yes, I will keep your secret safe. Now go and enjoy what is left of the day together."

As they walked away from the house, Missy told Mathew, "I knew my father would be glad for us."

Three weeks later, Mother Martha found a note on Charles' door. I read:

Dear Family,

I have gone to join the army. Please do not try to find me to bring me home. I have been wanting to do this for some time and feel it is my duty to my country to fight with my friends. I love you all and will write when I get to where I am going. Please pray for my safety."

Love,

Charles

When Abagail was told that Charles had gone to join the army, she cried and could not be comforted.

It was bad enough for Jonathan and Mathew to go, but now Charles, too, will be in harm's way," she cried.

As with all the country, the Williams homes were praying for the safe return of their loved ones.

Chapter 16:
Influenza Strikes

Winter is usually very cold in the northern states of the country, but this winter seemed to be extra harsh. No one could manage to stay warm. No one knew where the first case of influenza came from, but all at once it was there and it seemed that everyone had it.

Dr. Gohagen could not keep up with the terrible epidemic. He traveled from house to house until at last he became ill. Being a strong healthy man, he was able to overcome the disease and it seemed to make him more determined than ever to do as much as he could to treat the sick.

The Williams family was no exception. It began with a raspy throat, then fever and chills. Father had to brave the ice and snow to bring in wood for the fireplaces. They tried to huddle in the living room during the day and Charlene slept with Missy for warmth at night. The cook slept in a makeshift bed in the kitchen to keep the fire going there. Lots of warm blankets came out of the closet where they resided. Hot soups were the main stay for the family during the day, especially chicken soup. One night, cook made 'snow ice cream' with some of the snow left on part of the back porch. It made everyone so cold that they determined not to have that dessert again for a while.

Mother Martha came down with the dreaded 'flu' first. At breakfast that morning she felt warm to the touch. The doctor was called and came as soon as he could. By the time he got there, she was having chills and coughing a lot. The doctor gave her the medicine he was giving everyone else. He advised her to drink plenty of water, eat chicken soup and keep as warm as possible. After two more days, she began to talk to her dead parents, calling out to them to help her. She died three days later.

Theodore and Edwina made the long journey from New York. Because of the cold, they left their baby daughter, Patricia, back in their home in New York with her nursemaid. When they arrived, the rest of the family met them at the door and everyone cried together.

"I knew the flu was bad back here, but I never dreamed it was bad enough for people to die from it," wept Edwina. "What on earth will you all do without Mother Martha?"

"I do not know. I do not know!" cried Missy. "Father is beside himself and blames it on his not taking better care of her. The truth is that no one could have saved her. She had grown so frail worrying about Jonathan that she just could not fight it."

The undertaker came to the house and embalmed her body and laid her in a beautiful casket. It was set up in the living room and neighbors came and 'sat up' all night with the corpse, as was the custom in those days. Everyone brought food for the mourners, who were staying all night. Because of the weather, they decided to have the funeral there in the living room. The preacher came and gave the eulogy. Two of her friends sang 'Amazing Grace'. It had been her favorite song. The frozen ground made it difficult to dig the grave but the men managed to accomplish the chore. She was laid to rest in the Williams cemetery on the hill overlooking the farm.

Missy's Father could not be comforted. He sat with his head in his hands and kept saying, "Why could it not have been me? She was the one who held the home together. We had fifty-two wonderful years together. I loved her since we met at a dance at the church. Why could it not have been me? I do not want to live without her."

Within a week, Missy's father started having chills and fever. When Dr. Gohagen came, he looked very grave when he came out of the bedroom. He called Missy to one side and told her that her father was a very sick man and she would have to take over the household chores of bringing in wood for the fireplaces. "Can you and Charlene feed the horses and take care of the outside chores?" he asked.

"I will do my best," she replied. "Dr. Gohagen, I believe Abagail and the children should come out here to the farm and remain until this flu season is past, what do you think?"

The doctor nodded in agreement. "I will bring Abagail and the children out here as soon as I return to town, if she is willing," he said.

The doctor arrived with Abagail and the children that evening. She was glad to be with the rest of the family and volunteered to help with outside chores. Missy welcomed the extra help. Thank goodness there was a large woodpile to keep the fireplaces going. By this time, the women put another bed into Missy's bedroom and kept the fire in the fireplace going there. They brought down the twin's small beds from the attic and placed them in the large bedroom with the adults. They all stayed warm together.

When Edwina saw that her Father was becoming ill with the flu, she and Theodore decided to stay another week and help with the chores.

The fire in the bedroom where father and mother had slept had to be stoked during the night also. When her father got 'bad' Missy slept in a chair next to his bed.

Father Williams passed away during the night, two weeks after his beloved Martha died. Once again, the house was filled with friends who sat that night after the undertaker had done his job. As with Martha, the funeral was held there in the home and the ladies sang 'Amazing Grace'. He was laid to rest beside his beloved Martha in the cemetery on the hill.

The flu raged all through the town. Two and three people died every day. The undertaker ran out of caskets and had to make a trip to a neighboring town to find more. It was a terrible winter and those left prayed for Spring to come soon.

Abagail, Missy and Charlene talked often about the soldiers and wondered if their loved ones were safe. When a letter came from any of them, all three of them all read it over and over for comfort.

Theodore and Edwina felt they must return to New York to their small daughter. They left amid tearful goodbyes.

But there was more sadness to come

Three days later, there was a knock on the front door and upon unlocking the door, they found Jonathan on the other side. He was cold, and looked gaunt and tired.

Abagail ran to him and encircled him with her arms. "Oh Jonathan, how glad I am to see you. Get in here where it is warm and tell us about the war. Is it as bad as we have been hearing? Is the flu there, too? Oh, my darling how much weight have you lost since leaving? I just want to hold you close to me."

"My dear ones," began Jonathan. "I have the saddest of news to bring you. The reason I have returned today is to bring the body of our beloved Charles. He was mortally wounded and was brought to the makeshift hospital. There was nothing I could do to save the boy. I tried everything I could do, but to no avail. I brought him back home to be laid to rest in our cemetery where at least we can go and visit his grave. So many others were buried close to the battle ground."

"No! no!" cried Charlene. "Not Charles! Tell me you left him alive. Please Jonathan, tell me he is still back there and you came home for a visit. Please tell me Charles is still living back there. I cannot live and breathe if he is dead. I am begging you. Tell me he is alright." She was hysterical by this time and screaming the words at Jonathan.

Jonathan ran to her and caught her before she fainted and fell to the floor. He called to Missy to bring the smelling salts for him to help Charlene. When Charlene revived, she started screaming again. "Why did he have to go to that awful war? There is not a person there worth his little fingernail. Why did I not know he was going to slip off that night? Maybe I could have stopped him. Why did he feel it was his war? He was only fifteen years old and had a whole life ahead of him. Why did God let this happen to him? I do not understand why. He was the other half of my life. We were born together!!

Jonathan carried her to the couch and laid her down.

"Let me get something from the wagon that will calm you down and make you sleep," Jonathan told her. He quickly made his way to the wagon and returned with his medicine bag. After Missy had brought a glass of water, Charlene took the medicine that Jonathan gave her. Then she laid back down and closed her eyes and after a few minutes was asleep.

During all this time, the rest of those present were so shocked, they did not cry. Now the news finally hit them that Charles had died and his corpse was in the wagon. Shock turned to sorrow.

"Where are Mother and Father?" asked Jonathan.

"Oh Jonathan, you do not know," cried Abagail.

"Know what?" asked Jonathan.

"Both Mother and Father have died of the flu. We did not know how to get word to you that they had died. Edwina and Theodore came home for the funerals. They are buried beside each other up on the hill," Missy told her brother.

"Somehow I knew that all was not well here at home. I just had a feeling about it. Let me sit down and digest this news," said Jonathan. He sat very still for a few minutes. "Although this is a time for mourning for them also, we must prepare for Charles' funeral. I will get the undertaker. We cannot open the casket because of the condition of the body. It is best to remember Charles as he was before he left here to join the war."

So, the undertaker did his job and Charles' body was transferred from a wooden box to a beautiful casket. As usual, the neighbors came and sat with Charles all night.

Among the mourners who came to stay were Judge Amos Chandler and his wife Mary Lee. They were heartbroken for they loved Charles and Charlene as if the two-young people were their own children. Mary Lee kept saying, " If only we had known how determined he was to do his duty to the country, we might have talked him out of going to war so young. He was such a fine young man and we loved him so much." The Judge wept openly and would not be comforted. He told everyone he loved Charles as much as he would have loved his own son.

As for Abagail, she could not acknowledge Charles as her son. Although she tried to hide her heartbreaking sorrow, Missy knew the pain Abagail was going through. The agony of losing her first born son was almost too much for Abagail to bear. She asked to see Charles' body.

"You do not want to see him," said Jonathan.

"Yes, I do," said the sad Mother Abagail. "I need to know what happened to him."

Abagail finally won and Jonathan agreed to allow her to see Charles' body. The undertaker had done an excellent job of taking care of the body. When she was allowed to see him, she cried, "Oh Charles, why did you have to be killed?" She leaned over the body and kissed him on the forehead. She stood for a moment and looked at her baby then turned and walked away. Jonathan put his arm around her and helped her to a chair. Then he left and returned with something to ease her sobbing.

They did not notify Theodore and Edwina because of the harsh weather and the long journey they would have to make to attend the funeral. They received the news after the funeral was over.

Charles was buried in his uniform up on the hill beside Mother and Father Williams.

Chapter 17:
A Surprise Visit

When Missy left Dr. Gohagen's office, she was both happy and sad. She was happy to be carrying Mathew's baby, but sad because she had not heard from him for almost three months.

On her way home to the farm, she stopped to visit Abagail and see when the last time she had heard from Jonathan. Abagail was glad to report that she had a letter from him yesterday. He had not seen Mathew at all. Jonathan was not stationed even close to where Mathew had been last seen.

Missy traveled the road back to the farm. She was tired and just wanted to lie down. It would do her good to be by herself after the news of no news from Mathew. Charlene was gone over to visit the Judge and Mary Lee. They comforted each other during this period of sorrow over Charles' death. Agnes the cook had gone to town for supplies.

She had not been lying down for thirty minutes when there came a knock on the door.

Now who on earth could that be? The peddler who came three or four times a year had been there only last week and she was not expecting any of the neighbors.

She made her way to the door and asked, "Who's there?"

A man's voice came through the door, "Someone you have not seen in a long time."

Her curiosity got the best of her and she opened the door to find Abraham Dunbar, the man who used to be called the town bully.

"Well, hello, little Missy. Only you are not so little now, are you?" Abraham asked.

"What do you want?" asked Missy.

"Well now, I just want some food, a place to sleep for a few days and maybe a little loving from a pretty woman like you," he said.

"You are not welcome here. I know what you did to the barber. Now get out of here and go somewhere else to find food and a place to sleep," Missy told him.

"I have come all this way to find you. Tell me, how do you know about the barber? Were you there that night when he tried to deny he almost cut the sheriff's throat? Where were you hiding, little Missy?" he asked.

"I was hiding in one of the trees and saw it all. After you threw the barber in the river, Fisherman Joe jumped in and rescued him. Fisherman Joe turned out to be a doctor and set the arm you broke and sewed up his face. He and his wife and children left town because of you," Missy told him.

"That is just too bad. I hoped they would find his body on down the river," he jeered.

Missy tried to close the door, but he was too fast for her and stuck his boot in the doorway so the door would not close.

"Now that's no way to treat a friend, is it? I happen to know that no one else is at home so you better be nice to me and let me come in," he laughed.

Missy let the door fling open and ran to the stairs. She was more agile than he, so she made it to her Father's bedroom and locked the door from the inside.

"Oh ho! So, you want to play games, eh? Well, I can push this door down easily," he laughed. He made a run at the door and jarred it a little bit.

Missy knew where Father had kept his shotgun and she ran to the closet and got it. It was still loaded and she remembered how her father had taught her to shoot it.

"Get away from the door and leave or you will be sorry," she cried.

"Is that right? Well this time I will succeed in breaking the door down," he yelled.

Missy heard him take the run to break down the door and unlocked the door and opened it just as he was about to hit it. The huge man fell into the room and looked up into the barrel of the shotgun.

"I was not kidding when I said you would be sorry for trying to break down the door," Missy told him.

"You do not have the guts to shoot a man," he snarled.

"Do you want to take a chance on that?" she asked.

"Why, yes, I will," he yelled as he got up and started toward her. She raised the shotgun and pulled the trigger hitting him squarely in the chest. He fell at her feet and drew three more breaths before he died.

Missy ran to the barn, saddled a horse and rode as fast as she could to the sheriff's office. There she told the sheriff about what had happened at the farm.

The sheriff, the undertaker (who was also the coroner) and Dr. Gohagen all followed Missy back to the farm where they found the dead man.

The sheriff began to question Missy as if he did not believe her.

"How did you know this man? How did he know to come here to find food and shelter? Why did you let him in the house if you knew of his bad character? How did you know about the gun? Why did you shoot him?" the sheriff asked her.

"Now, just a minute, sheriff," It was Dr. Gohagen who spoke. "I am very familiar with this man and he was capable of doing great harm to this young lady. Before you came to town, he was known as the town bully. When I lived in the shack down by the river close to the cave, I saw this man beat up several men and throw them into the river. I was able to rescue all of them and nurse them back to health. Missy watched me rescue a barber and set an arm this man had broken and sew up his face where someone had hit and cut his face. Missy is very lucky that she knew where her father's shotgun was hidden and that she knew how to use it. Do not think for a minute that she did not have to defend herself."

"Dr. Gohagen, I respect your position and believe you could be telling the truth, but I feel we should have a hearing on this matter," said the sheriff.

"You are the sheriff," said Dr. Gohagen.

Since we only have her word, I am arresting her. I have spoken to Judge Harner and he has set her bail at one thousand dollars," the sheriff told Dr. Gohagen.

"She probably does not have that much money on hand, so I will pay the bail," said Dr. Gohagen. "But it will take a couple of days for me to transfer funds from New York to the local bank."

"Then she will only be in jail for a couple of days," said the sheriff.

So, Missy was taken to jail until the good doctor could get the funds for her release.

Missy was having morning sickness and the food at the jail did nothing to improve her feelings of being pregnant.

On the first morning, she had a visitor. Charlene came and brought a letter to Missy that looked very important. It was from the Division of the Army. Missy opened it with trembling fingers and this is the message it brought:

Dear Mrs. Mathew Morgan,

We regret to inform you that your husband, Mathew Morgan is missing in action.

Sincerely Yours,

General John Goetz

"No, no, it cannot be true. I am in jail and accused of murder and now Mathew is missing in action. I cannot bear it. Dear God, what else can happen?" cried Missy.

Charlene tried to comfort her. "God will take care of you and he will take care of Mathew. At least the letter did not say that Mathew is dead. That would be the worst news. Please try to be patient. I know that is easy to say, but I just know things will be alright," she said.

Missy hugged Charlene and promised to try to have faith, but she was beginning to have her doubts.

Chapter 18:
The Trial and Death of the Judge

On the second day, Dr. Gahagan's money arrived at the local bank and he paid the one thousand dollars for Missy to go free from jail. She was never so glad to get back to the farm house. The cook and Charlene had cleaned the rug where the town bully had bled and everything looked back to normal. But things were not normal.

Dr. Gohagen had hired an attorney from New York to defend Missy and the man appeared to know what he was doing.

The next Sunday, Missy decided to miss going to church, but Charlene went and sat in the Williams' pew by herself. After church, Mathew's mother approached Charlene.

"I just wanted to tell you how sorry I am that you are having to face all the gossip and whispering since your sister, Missy, killed that man. I am sure you are ashamed of her. I am so glad we were able to get Mathew away from her. He seemed to have a rather high regard for her," the woman said condescendingly.

"Do not waste your sympathy on me, Mrs. Morgan," said Charlene sweetly. "Apparently you do not know that Mathew and Missy have been secretly married for some time. He came back to the farm and they were married in the middle of the night. She has been wrongly accused of murder. It was self-defense. She is pregnant with your first grandchild right now. The worst part about it is that she received a letter from the War Department yesterday that Mathew is missing in action. If I were you, I would be rethinking some of the gossip that is going around and try to help Missy when she gives birth to your grandchild." Charlene lifted her chin and walked away leaving Mrs. Morgan standing with her mouth open.

Missy could not believe that she was being accused of murder. The attorney assured her that the trial would not last very long and she would be acquitted but people in town looked at her then turned their heads and walked on.

A jury was selected and the Judge opened the trial.

Missy's attorney called eight witnesses to testify as to her good character and to tell the jury that in no way could Missy have committed the crime of murder.

The blacksmith took the stand and said that he felt that Abraham Dunbar would not have tried to harm Missy and she had no right to shoot him. He said, "I knew Abraham Dunbar was a fair and honest man. I knew him when he still lived here in town. He might have been a little rough to some folks, but he actually was as gentle as a lamb."

The jury looked at each other and nodded their heads. It did not look too good for Missy.

Both Missy's attorney and the prosecutor gave their closing arguments and the jury was given instructions by the judge when the back door to the court room was flung open and a man about five feet five inches tall strode into the court room.

"Hold everything," he shouted. "That girl did shoot Abraham Dunbar in self-defense. I know because I was there and heard and saw the whole thing. Put me on the witness stand and I will tell you what happened that day."

The judge ordered the court to swear the man in.

I rode with Abraham Dunbar for a while and had just about decided that I did not want to be associated with him anymore, but he threatened to kill me if I left him. He said he knew some folks that had a lot of money and they would give us food and lodging for free. I believed him. When we got there, I could tell that he was not welcomed at the house and I watched as he pushed himself in the front door. I got off my horse and went up on the porch to tell him to leave the pretty lady alone. Then I saw her run up the stairs and he follow her and threaten to break down the door. Then she opened the door and asked him to leave or she would shoot. He cursed her and made a lunge for her. She had no choice but to shoot him. I did not want to get involved in this mess, but I could not stand by and let an innocent woman be hanged for something she did not do. I have already sworn on the Bible, but I swear on my mother's grave that I am telling the truth."

Once again, the attorney and the prosecutor gave closing arguments and the judge gave instructions to the jury.

The jury was only out for twenty minutes and came back with a verdict of "Not Guilty."

Missy, Charlene and Abagail all got up and thanked the man over and over. He apologized for not coming forward sooner.

Missy's attorney said to her, "Without that man's testimony, I am afraid we were headed for trouble."

As they started out of the court room, Mrs. Morgan stepped out of the seating area and faced Missy.

"Am I to understand that you are married to my son?" she asked.

"Yes, Mathew and I are married," Missy told the woman.

Charlene got between Missy and Mrs. Morgan. "You have no right to talk to Missy after the way you have tried to smear her good name. Leave her alone and do not bother her. She has been through a lot these last few days."

"Mathew must have loved you very much," said Mrs. Morgan. "We were just trying to protect our only son and keep him from making a mistake. It seems we are the ones who have made the mistake. When you are feeling better, Missy, can we talk?"

"I am very tired right now. There will be more time in the future for talk. Right now, I just want to go home and rest for a week," Missy told Mathew's mother. With that said, Missy turned and walked out the door with Charlene and Abagail.

When Missy and Charlene arrived at home, there was an urgent message for them. The Judge, Amos Chandler was very ill and wanted them to come to his home as soon as they could get there.

They took the carriage to the judge's home. Several people were there including Dr. Gohagen. When they stepped inside the door, he motioned for them to come to the judge's bedroom. The doctor shook his head.

"Oh, I am so glad to see you both," the Judge said. Charlene, I wanted to tell you how very much I have enjoyed having both you and Charles visit our home during the past years. It almost seems as if you two belonged to Mary Lee and me. I guess I mourned Charles' death almost as much as you did. The doctor says there is nothing more he can do for me, so I want to tell you how much I have loved you and your brother. Please take care of Mary Lee for me. She will need your strong spirit and good heart to help her. I hope you will remember me kindly in the coming years."

"I love you and Mary Lee, too," cried Charlene. "I promise to take care of Mary Lee. You two have almost been like mine and Charles' parents since our own parents died. Now, rest, and I will return tomorrow."

As she turned to leave, the Judge asked her, "Can you not stay longer? Mary Lee will need someone to stay with her if something happens with me."

"Of course, I will stay if you need me to," cried Charlene. She sat down by his bedside and held his hand for a long time. Mary Lee sat on the other side.

At ten thirty that same night, the Judge passed away. Charlene was so glad she stayed to comfort Mary Lee. She and Missy spent the night there and returned home the next morning.

Charlene hoped that this would be the last death in the family, (For she considered the Judge to be family) for a long time.

But she did not get to see him again, for he passed away that night at ten o'clock.

Chapter 19:
The Return and the Truth

The long, dreadful, awful war was finally over.

Jonathan rode home with a heavy heart. The war took so many young men to their deaths or left them with missing arms and legs. He became a surgeon in the makeshift hospital tents because of necessity not of training. The worst part of operating was when they ran out of medication and the pain was almost unbearable for the soldiers. He had nightmares or else could not sleep at night because he could not save more lives. Jonathan did not want to accept the plaque given to him by the president. He felt all the men who fought and died deserved it more than he did.

When he arrived home, he found that Abagail was very ill. Dr. Gohagen was puzzled as to her diagnosis. She had the symptoms of the stomach flu, vomiting and diarrhea and could not keep anything in her stomach. Even water would not stay down. She had had the condition for almost two weeks and was very weak and had headaches along with the other illness. Jonathan was puzzled also. He stayed with her for two days then felt he should go and check on Missy.

Missy met him at the door and threw her arms around him and gave him a bear hug.

"I am so glad to see you," Missy said. "Come on in and I will give you an update on the condition of the farm."

After Jonathan was seated at the dining room table, Missy began to give him the run down on what had taken place while he was away.

"I have rented all of the five hundred acres to the Amish farmers locally. So far, they have done an excellent job of raising the crops. Last spring was wet so they were late getting the crops planted but had good luck with planting and harvesting the crops. I had to put a new roof on the barn and the house. I sold all the cattle because we, Charlene and me, could not take care of them. We were able to keep all the horses and feed them and kept them ridden and used to pulling the wagon and carriage. Agnes the cook decided that she wanted to return to her home in Alabama so Charlene and I are learning to cook," she laughed. Then she grew serious. "Did you see my Mathew in all your travel? I received a letter from the War Department telling me he was missing in action."

"No, I have not seen Mathew. There was a southern prison that was so bad that a lot of men died there. I did not try to go and help them because I was afraid they would hold me there also," he told her. "I cannot leave Abagail for too long because she is so sick. I know that sounds funny since I have been away for so long, but I feel she needs me right now more than ever," he told her.

"I did not realize she was so ill. Charlene and I will be in town shortly to come and visit her," said Missy.

About that time, Molly Anne waddled into the room.

"And just who is this little beautiful doll?" queried Jonathan.

"Hi! I am Molly Anne. Who are you?" she asked Jonathan.

Missy looked fondly at her daughter. "Why this is your Uncle Jonathan," she said.

"You mean to tell this is your and Mathew's daughter?" asked Jonathan. "Well, I will be a monkey's uncle!"

"No, you are my uncle, silly," laughed Molly Anne. She ran to Jonathan and climbed onto his lap. "You may hug and kiss me on the cheek now," she said.

Jonathan drew her close and kissed her little pink cheek. Then he put her off his lap and left to go home to Abagail.

That evening late, there was a knock on the front door. Since the last man came to the door, Missy kept it padlocked and was careful to go to the window and see who was on the front porch.

The knock was insistent and continued to sound. Missy went to the window to see who would be there at that time of evening.

When she saw who was on the other side of the door, she screamed and ran and opened the door! For on the other side of the door was her beloved Mathew!

"A little cautious, are you not?" Mathew asked. He was leaning on a pair of crutches and looked as if he might fall at any moment.

Missy almost knocked him down as she threw her arms around him held him close to kiss his parched lips and told him over and over how much she loved him and missed him. He was filthy dirty, but it made no difference to her.

"Come in, come in," she cried. "I have prayed so long for the moment you would come home. I still cannot believe you are here. Why are you on crutches, Mathew?"

"All in good time, after I catch my breath," Mathew told her. "First let me rest and get a bath and shave so I can look presentable."

Once again, Molly Anne came running into the room and stopped short. She ran to Missy and asked, "Who is that awful smelling man, Mama? I do not like him."

Missy gathered Molly Anne in her arms. "This is no awful smelling man. Molly Anne, meet your father."

"I do not have a father. He is in the war and did not come back home to us," Molly Anne said.

Tears came to Mathew's eyes as he said to Missy, "In all the time I was in that prison camp, I thought of you, but I never dreamed I had left you with a babe. She is such a beautiful child. What is her name?"

"My name is Molly Anne," she said. "What is a prison camp?"

"It is a very bad place to go to," answered Mathew.

"We have been so busy talking, I know you must be itching to have a bath, shave and get fresh clothes," said Missy.

Afterwards Mathew donned fresh clothing and they had some dinner.

"You look and smell a lot better," Molly Anne told her father.

Charlene returned from Mary Ann's house and could not believe that Mathew had returned. She was so happy to see him. They all talked into the night, catching up on what had happened at the farm and listening to Mathew tell of what had happened to him. He had been in prison for almost three years and had almost starved to death. When the war ended, some of the other soldiers helped him to get back to the farm or he would have died in the south with other prisoners. Mathew did not know that Charles had been killed in the war.

Next morning, at the breakfast table, Missy told them of how sick Jonathan had said Abagail was and that they needed to go to see about her. So, they all loaded into the carriage and made the trip to town.

When they arrived, Jonathan met them at the door and said, "I am so glad you are here Charlene. She has been asking for you."

Charlene and Missy went into Abagail's bedroom where she looked very pale and ill. Abagail asked them to sit down.

"I trust that what I am about to reveal will not go farther than the walls of this bedroom," Abagail began.

"If that is your wish, we will do as you say," said both Charlene and Missy.

"Alright," said Abagail. "Missy do you remember when your mother was pregnant? Well, she was not pregnant, I was. She wore a pillow to pretend and I stayed in my room because everyone would know that I was really the one who was going to have a baby."

"Yes, I knew mother was not pregnant. I was in the living room and heard mother and father talking about it," said Missy.

"Your mother and father were angels. I was raped and that is the reason I was pregnant," said Abagail. "I cannot go to my grave without telling you, Charlene, this secret. I would not have told you while he was still living, but he is now deceased," Abagail told them.

"Who was the man?" asked Charlene.

"Judge Amos Chandler was the man and you and Charles were the twins born to me. Charlene, you are my daughter and I am so proud of you. Now, therefore I asked you both not to tell this. It would ruin my marriage to Jonathan, I am afraid. Your real name should be Charlene Chandler. I am asking that you never reveal my secret," said Abagail.

"So, you are really my mother? Judge Chandler is my father? Right now, I hate him and love him at the same time. Hate him for causing you so much pain and love him for all the kindness and love he showed to me and Charles. Now, things become clearer. He was so distraught when Charles was killed. He must have guessed that we were his children. How did you ever go through losing Charles and pretend he was only Jonathan's brother? It must have broken your heart. Oh, Mother, I wish I had known this before. I would have treated you so differently. Please get well soon. You and I have a lot of catching up to do," cried Charlene.

"I feel better already, Charlene. This secret has taken its toll on me during the years when I wanted so badly to claim both of you as my own," Abagail told her daughter.

It was Missy's turn to speak. "I knew the twins belonged to you, Abagail, but I would never have dreamed that Judge Amos Chandler was the father and that he had raped you," she said.

"I never should have agreed to go for a walk with him and I flirted unmercifully with him. Looking back, he probably assumed I wanted the incident to happen. I was a silly young girl at the time. I have paid dearly for that mistake the rest of my life," said Abagail.

"Please go now and let me rest. Come again to visit me and let's catch up on many things, Charlene," said Abagail.

"I promise that I shall," answered Charlene as she hugged her mother.

Missy and Charlene left the room and went outside to join the others in the living room.

"Could I borrow a horse from you," Charlene asked Jonathan. "I need to do an errand for Mary Ann Chandler."

"Of course, you may," answered Jonathan. "How is Abagail doing?"

"I believe she is going to get well," said Missy. "She seemed to perk up after our visit."

Charlene rode with the wind until she arrived at Mary Ann's house. She was breathless as she knocked on the front door.

"Come in, Charlene," Mary Ann told her. "You look as if you have ridden quite fast to get here quickly. Is anything wrong?"

Charlene put her arms around her good friend and gave her a big bear hug.

"There is something I have to ask you," said Charlene.

"Oh, dear, I believe I know the question and the answer is 'yes'," answered Mary Ann.

"How long have your known?" asked Charlene.

"Please sit down and I will tell you," said Mary Ann. "About a week before he passed away, Amos called me to his bedside and asked my forgiveness. I asked him 'whatever for?'. He told me of the incident that happened with your mother. He had counted up the months from the time it happened and became sure of it when he looked at you and your brother. His mother had blonde hair like Charles and when the judge was young, his hair was red like yours. After he determined that you two belonged to him, he talked to me about having you two over to our home and trying to be as nice to you as we could be. He wanted to make it up to you for the incident. Of course, not having children of our own, I readily agreed and we have loved you both so very much. It is my sincere hope and prayer that you will find it in your heart to forgive him for what he did."

"I forgive him now as we speak," Charlene told her. "I hope I can still come and visit you as I promised him that I would do and take care of you."

"Thank you, Charlene. I look forward to having you visit me and taking care of me," Mary Ann told her. "One more thing. Since we had no heirs, we decided to leave all our property and money to you. It will help you in your future whatever you decide to do."

Charlene was speechless for a moment. "You did not need to do that. I would have taken care of you anyway," she said. "I need to go now, but I will return within the hour and spend the rest of the day with you."

She rode the horse to the cemetery where the Judge had been laid to rest, climbed down and walked to the Judge's grave.

"I am sorry I did not know you were my real father although, looking back, I now realize that I loved you as if you had been my real father. Thank you for being so kind to Charles and me. I only regret that Charles will never know who you really are. I know he loved you as much as I did. I will keep my promise to you that I will care for Mary Ann. And I will come to visit you often," she promised him.

Her tears fell on his tombstone as she placed a small stone on the top of it.

Made in the USA
Columbia, SC
02 November 2017